Autumn Secrets

A Katana Bay Series

Katie Winters

D1522118

Chapter One

"You are not your past, Nancy. You are here, on Martha's Vineyard, with me. My children will be your children; my home is your home. The darkness you've left behind will remain far away from you. And with me and the love we've built together, you will find peace."

Neal had spoken these words the night before their wedding, twelve years before. They had stood out on the back porch of his mansion, a house far bigger than anything Nancy had ever envisioned, even in her wildest dreams, and he'd taken her delicate hands in his firm, soft ones and whispered this mantra, just loud enough for only her to hear. Inside the house, family members and new yet dear friends on the island had drunk and laughed together in celebration of Neal and Nancy having found one another.

Neal had known the inner chaos of Nancy's soul. It was something she'd revealed to him early on, when she had first met him in Bangkok. He'd floated the idea of her coming back to the Katama Lodge and Wellness Spa to

1

work alongside him and his dear daughter, Elsa. At the time, there had been a low yet constant sizzle between them. A sense that maybe if Nancy could get over all her inner anxieties and fears of commitment, she could find love in this great, confident, and eternally honest man— a man who had been through so many hardships of his own throughout the years.

After all, he'd lost his wife. He'd lost his son. His ex-wife, Karen, had been a manipulative woman, so hungry for his money that she had used some very disgusting language toward his daughters and split them up for decades. He'd laid out his entire life before her, showed all his cards upfront, and slowly but surely, Nancy had revealed her truth.

The truth she'd had a baby at the age of sixteen. That Janine no longer spoke to her because she had abandoned her and fled New York City. That she'd struggled with just about everything there was to struggle with: money, alcohol, and men, to name a few. It had never occurred to Nancy to even ask the universe for some kind of second chance.

Not that Neal had been a second chance. He had been like the twenty-first chance in a world that seemed apt to take Nancy under and keep her there. Neal had fished her out of the darkness. He'd been her beacon of light, and she'd embraced it with everything she had. This had been a gift that she would not turn her back on.

And then, eight months ago in January, he had passed on from this world and into the next.

The heartache in the wake of his death had been monstrous. It still lived as a horrible weight on her heart. She had truly loved him like no other.

Now with her eyelids closed and her legs bent

beneath her, she heard her voice illustrate the next moves in her six a.m. yoga class at the Katama Lodge and Wellness Spa. It was mid-September, and ten women from all walks of life, from all ranges of heartaches and horrors, had come together to turn their eyes toward Nancy like she was some kind of healer.

If only they knew how broken she really was.

This had been the funny thing about that journalist's article the previous month. Carmella, one of Nancy's stepdaughters, had given a journalist she'd been romantically involved with quite a bit of information about the family. Afterward, he had written a damning article, stating that the Katama Lodge and Wellness Spa couldn't possibly heal any of its guests, specifically when the workers themselves were women in the midst of their own heartache, divorce, and substance.

Nancy had been angry with the journalist who tried to defame their good name, what Neal had worked so hard to build. But she'd also recognized the glowing truth of it.

"You are not your past." She said this to the women in the yoga studio now, echoing what Neal had said all those years ago. "Say it with me, ladies. You are not your past."

"You are not your past." Each of the women murmured it— from the forty-something blond woman who resembled Gwyneth Paltrow off to the left to the voluptuous woman with dark curls in the back. Even the scrawny twentysomething, who had recently informed Nancy that she'd come to the Katama Lodge and Wellness Spa to get over her trust fund boyfriend running away with her sister.

The stories Nancy heard while at the Katama Lodge could have filled countless books. Her own story seemed wildly inventive and dense, with countless variations and bends in the road. Neal had said this, too: that she'd lived far more lives than he ever had. To this, Nancy had simply said she was exhausted.

"Now, open your eyes, ladies. Inhale. Exhale. Inhale. Exhale." Nancy's own eyes scanned just above the women's heads. It was far too aggressive to make eye contact before seven in the morning. "Thank you for a remarkable first hour of the morning. As you continue your journey here at the Katama Lodge and Wellness Spa, I hope that you uphold your sense of purpose and your promise for a new chapter. Enjoy the rest of your day, and I hope to see you soon."

* * *

Twenty minutes later, Nancy stood in her yoga outfit in the large kitchen space just down the hall from her yoga studio. The kitchen staff buzzed around her. There was the slicing sound of the knife against the onion and the sizzle of the garlic in the skillet. Bright tomatoes bulged in large wooden bowls, and the chef rattled out commands. Nancy continued to add elements to the blender for the perfect green smoothie she was preparing for herself: berries, spirulina, ice, with a bit of vegan protein and a half of a banana. She buzzed the high-grade blender for twenty seconds, and it spat out a cup of nutrients.

"Morning, Nancy," the chef said as she poured her green smoothie. "You good?"

"Another beautiful day," Nancy returned.

"You always say that. Where do you get all that optimism from?"

Nancy laughed lightly. "If only you'd met me thirty

years ago. I would have had forty-seven things to complain about."

"Guess I should do more yoga," the chef replied.

Nancy padded out from the kitchen and headed toward the porch, where she wrapped a blanket around her shoulders and gazed out across the shimmering waters of Katama Bay. This was how she liked to start her day: meditation, yoga, a green juice, then a thoughtful time there on the porch lost in her thoughts. In previous years, Neal had joined her for this contemplative time. She had never told him before how much it had mesmerized her that she'd found someone she could sit silently with. He had been such a calm presence while demanding nothing of her. And in the wake of this emotion, she had given him everything she'd been able to.

Again, a sudden headache banged away in the back of her skull. She closed her eyes as another wave of fatigue struck her. This had been a rather frequent conundrum the past few months. She couldn't fully pinpoint when it had all begun— perhaps around the time that she'd called Janine back to her. That had been such a flurry of emotion, a wildly confusing time, that she'd hardly even noticed her health ailments.

Now, the headaches and fatigue were all hitting her more and more frequently. It had become something she couldn't ignore any longer.

The doctor's office receptionist answered on the third ring. Nancy asked if she could arrange an appointment that week. The doctor's office was quite small; her doctor had very few clients as he was semi-retired. The receptionist told her it wouldn't be a problem.

"What about tomorrow afternoon?"

Nancy agreed. Just as she finalized the time, Janine

appeared on the other side of the porch door. She held her version of a green smoothie sans the banana. As she pressed open the door, she grinned broadly at her mother. "Hi there. You look comfy out here."

Nancy still couldn't quite get over it. Every time Janine greeted her so warmly, she was reminded of a long-ago version of Janine: perhaps age four or five, when she'd woken Nancy up almost exclusively by jumping on the bed with excitement for a brand-new day. Nancy had been twenty at the time— just a child herself, quite groggy, and frequently coming off a hangover. She hadn't fully appreciated that bright light of youthful energy. Probably, she'd asked Janine to quiet down.

You are not your past, she told herself now. She could practically hear Neal whispering it into her ear.

"Join me!" Nancy said sweetly as she shoved her phone back into her pocket.

Janine slipped into the chair beside her and nodded toward the view. "I don't know if I'll ever get over it. I wish I could sit out here all day and just stare across the water."

"Big schedule today?"

"Quite a few clients, yes," Janine affirmed. "After Lola's article, Elsa added a few more guests. We're filled up, and gosh, with the wedding coming up this weekend, I'm up to my ears in stress."

Nancy brought her hand over Janine's on the table and cupped it gently. At fifty-nine and forty-three, it was a strange thing to see them together, side by side like this. Frequently, people assumed they were sisters. Nancy hadn't considered what this era of their lives would be like. Long ago, she'd just seen a hungry toddler, then a child who'd needed her far more than Nancy had been able to be there.

"The wedding. Gosh, I just can't wait," Nancy said, forcing a smile.

"The girls are thrilled to have the wedding here on the Vineyard," Janine told her. "It was a whirlwind change, but Maggie wouldn't hear of anything else. And that Charlotte Hamner has been a remarkable wedding planner."

"She's quite good," Nancy agreed. "She's planned several elaborate weddings on this island in the past."

Nancy's words seemed somehow far away, even from herself. She furrowed her brow and felt another wave of fatigue fall over her. Janine's eyes flickered.

"You okay, Mom?"

Nancy nodded and took another sip of her smoothie. "Yes, of course."

"Okay." Janine's phone began to buzz. The name read "Maggie," Janine's eldest and the bride-to-be. "I guess there's another fire to put out. I'll see you later?"

"Good luck."

Janine stood from the chair and greeted her daughter warmly. "Hi, honey. How is everything?"

Mom.

It had taken Janine some real time to call Nancy "Mom" in the weeks after she had arrived at the Vineyard. Theirs had been an incredibly unique journey of understanding their past trauma, healing, and forgiveness.

And now, in the wake of whatever health issue she was facing, Nancy worried within in the depths of her soul that now that she'd just brought Janine back into her life, God forbid, she would be diagnosed with something serious. That alone would kill her.

"Please," Nancy breathed as her eyes closed. "Please. Just let me stay here with Janine, Maggie, and Alyssa a little longer. I only just got them back."

She'd been given the greatest gift— a second chance with her family. She wanted to laugh with them and gossip with them and celebrate everything from the wedding that weekend to births, birthdays, and graduations and on and into time itself. Nancy needed that like we need our hearts to beat.

Janine returned inside and stepped past the front desk, where Mallory stood in conversation with Elsa, her mother. The two looked remarkably similar, even down to the little ways they held their heads the slightest bit crooked when they listened intently. Mallory explained her mother's schedule for the morning prior to her approaching lunch with Bruce— an attorney she'd recently met and begun dating.

He had helped her out a great deal when she'd discovered that people attempted to take advantage of her and smear her deceased husband's name through the mud. Nancy had come to like Bruce. He was a solid man, contemplative and honest, with a tender heart that seemed open to the idea of Elsa's love.

"Oh, lunch with Bruce?" Nancy teased as she headed toward her office.

"Don't you start." Elsa's grin was electric.

"Just saying. Mallory, let me know if this woman's work ethic dies out as she nurses this crush of hers," Nancy said playfully. "We can't afford to lose revenue just because of some handsome attorney."

"I'll let you know," Mallory returned with a laugh.

"I'm not a teenager. I think I can control myself." Elsa tapped her hands on her hips.

"Yeah. You say that now. But the minute you look into Bruce's big, beautiful eyes—" Nancy tried.

"What's going on out here?" Carmella stepped out of her office. Her smile faltered the slightest bit at the sight of Nancy.

"They're giving me grief about my lunch with Bruce," Elsa told her. "Can you believe them? I can't catch a break."

Carmella chuckled. "We'd better watch her like a hawk."

"See? We've got Aunt Carmella on our side," Mallory pointed out.

Elsa and Carmella shared vibrant smiles. Nancy's fell. She was thrilled that the two Remington girls had begun to shift the pieces of their broken relationship and figure out new ways to heal. But as she'd always been tremendously close with Elsa and never found common ground with Carmella, Nancy wasn't entirely sure where she fit in with them.

In recent months, Nancy had felt her temper rise when they had torn into one another. "You two are sisters. You need to find a way to get along." Nancy was one to talk. She had struggled with animosity in her previous life and endless darkness, much like Carmella had.

But why wasn't she always willing to share this side of herself with Carmella? Perhaps it would unite them more. Maybe Carmella would sense Nancy's empathy toward her situation. Perhaps she would understand all the love that echoed through Nancy's soul.

Even now, as Nancy attempted to make eye contact with Carmella, her eyes fluttered away from her. Elsa cleared her throat and smacked her palms together. "Let's get started on another successful day at the Lodge, shall we?" Then Mallory perched in the receptionist chair, and Nancy took her cue: return to the yoga studio. Bend her way through the next hours. Remind so many other women that they weren't their past — not at all — even while she felt herself carry the dark burden of her own so immensely.

Chapter Two

I t was initially difficult for Nancy to find free time for her doctor's appointment. As the head massage therapist and yoga instructor, her schedule was jam-packed, tightly calibrated for her to see as many Katama guests as possible during their very strict health-oriented schedule, which Janine herself drew up. She and Mallory pieced through the online calendar and rearranged her appointments for the following morning and afternoon. Only once did Mallory ask, "What do you need the after-noon off for?" And only once had Nancy answered, "I have a few important errands to run for the wedding." This seemed like an appropriate answer. After all, Janine ran around like a chicken with her head cut off most mornings— absolutely frantic about Maggie's approaching big day.

Nancy drove with the windows down to Dr. Morgan's office. In her recent bi-annual checkups, Dr. Morgan had always called her a "portrait of health." "You'll be skipping and jumping well into your eighties, I imagine," he'd said once. She had thanked her lucky stars that all the heavy drinking and unhealthy lifestyle hadn't caught up with her.

Perhaps it finally had— many years after she'd cleaned up her act. That was how life went. It always nabbed you when you least expected it.

En route to the doctor's office, Janine called her. Without hesitation, Nancy answered it with the speaker-phone within her car, then immediately felt a stab of regret.

"Hey, Mom! I meant to catch you for lunch, but you're not here? Mallory said you stepped out?"

Nancy's throat nearly closed. After a strange pause, she burst out with, "Oh, yeah. I have a few errands to run. Just out and about."

"Ah. Okay. I told you to tell me about any errands you need me to run for the house, remember? I know the wedding's coming up, and I'm a bit of a mess, but I can still do things like pick up groceries. At least, I think I can."

Nancy's laughter rang false and strange. "Don't worry about it, honey. You have enough on your plate with the chaos this weekend. Alyssa and Maggie arrive here Thursday?"

"That's right," Janine affirmed. "And, I guess, Maxine and Jack as well."

Nancy groaned. Maxine was Janine's lifelong best friend. She had immigrated to the United States from France and never really lost that fantastic French allure. In their youths, Janine and Maxine had been perpetually attached at the hip. When Nancy had skipped town— a wild and debaucherous woman on the edge of sanity, even at the age of thirty-four, Maxine and Janine had moved in together and fought the wild world of Brooklyn on their own.

But over the summer, Janine had discovered the torturous fact that her dear best friend and her beloved husband had been having an affair. When Nancy had first read about this in a tabloid, she'd struggled to find words as she sensed the pain her daughter was wrapped up in. "How could Maxine do this to Janine?" she'd whispered to Elsa at the time.

Elsa, who hadn't been in Brooklyn thirty years ago, hadn't fully understood the drama of the question at hand. Instead, she had just gripped Nancy's hand as Nancy had said, "It's time for Janine to come back to me. It's time for us to find forgiveness. Finally."

"Maggie told Jack he couldn't bring Maxine," Janine explained. "But of course, he said he was the one paying for the wedding, and he would bring whoever he pleased. I suppose he's right to some extent, but gosh. He should think about his daughter for once. I wouldn't want such drama at my wedding."

"You know I don't know this man," Nancy said tenderly. "I know you loved him for so many years. And I also know that I want to run him over with my car a few times."

Janine's laughter was vibrant. Nancy could feel the tears behind it. It wasn't like you just got over your first love. It wasn't like Janine would ever fully get over this enormous betrayal. Even Henry, Janine's newfound documentarian boyfriend, whom Nancy and the others in the family adored, couldn't take that pain away. It colored everything else.

"And Maxine?" Janine asked then.

Nancy had reached the doctor's office. She parked in

the lot and leaned her head against the seat, her eyes closed. There it was again: another wave of fatigue.

"I don't want to run Maxine over with my car," Nancy admitted. "But I guess I wouldn't mind chopping off all her hair. And telling her just how little we believed her accent."

"Right? I mean, she's been in America for decades," Janine said. "She must really lean into it to make it that strong."

Nancy buzzed her lips. It was time for her to enter the office and face the music. In every way, she wanted to remain in that car, swapping half insults with her dearest daughter—anything to take away the root of her pain.

"I have to go, honey," she said finally.

"Ah. Right. I do, too. But I'll see you at home later?"

"I'll be the one with the Pinot Grigio," Nancy told her.

"Noted," Janine returned.

Nancy's entire body quivered as she entered the receptionist area. The woman at the desk flashed a smile that showed her adult braces. Nancy greeted her as warmly as possible, then sat at the edge of her chair and waited for Dr. Morgan to step out of his office. She half expected him to pronounce her as having only six weeks to live the moment he spotted her. But instead, he just greeted her in that familiar friendly manner of his, asked about her daughters and the Lodge, and then questioned her about her emotional health in the wake of Neal's death.

Dr. Morgan had been Neal's doctor, too, for a while

before he had transferred him over. Was Nancy supposed to blame this man for Neal's early death? Perhaps she should change doctors. This only occurred to her now, awkwardly in his presence. She brightened her smile and continued to answer his questions until he finally asked her why the heck she'd decided to schedule an appointment.

Nancy's words were delicate. She described her headaches, the pains, the wave after wave of fatigue, and, of course, the anxiety surrounding each episode.

"Is this something you've discussed with your daughters?" Dr. Morgan asked her, his brow furrowed.

"I want to keep it under wraps. Until we know for sure what any of this is."

Dr. Morgan nodded and furrowed his brow more, which resulted in a big vein bulging out across the side of his forehead.

"Plus, you've probably heard about the wedding we're about to have in the family." Nancy forced her voice to brighten. "It's all anyone can think about, including me. I just thought that maybe I should get these things checked out."

Dr. Morgan nodded. "Of course. I'm glad you did."

Nancy struggled reading his tone. Was he worried? Did he think she was overreacting? The last thing she wanted to do was make a big deal out of nothing. There was so much other stuff to think about.

"We should do a series of tests, I think," Dr. Morgan continued. "I can arrange them as early as this Thursday."

Nancy's heart dropped slightly in her chest. "Wow, that soon."

"Better to get ahead of anything," he continued.

"What do you imagine it is?"

"It's difficult to say. Your symptoms are representative of several ailments."

Nancy felt herself nod as he continued to speak. He outlined the tests he wanted to order and what she needed to do prior to each one. He then brought out several pamphlets with instructions for the tests, which featured smiling people who seemed ill-prepared for such terrifying illnesses. Who were the models for these pamphlets? Did they know they were featured in doctor's offices like this, probably all over the United States of America?

Nancy felt herself thank Dr. Morgan. She collected her purse and wandered out into the reception area to finalize the schedule for her tests. She then floated like a ghost back to her car, where she promptly burst into tears. Almost the minute she turned on her vehicle, the speaker system blared with a call from Janine.

"Hey, Mom! I wondered what happened to you."

"I'm still out running errands." Nancy's voice wavered dangerously.

"Ugh. Well, I wanted to tell you what happened with the flower girls' dresses because it's a complete nightmare."

Nancy said all the right things as she drove the car back to the Katama Lodge. She laughed and groaned and said, "That's insane," without ever feeling fully conscious of where the conversation had led her.

"Are you headed home soon, then?" Janine finally asked after the drama had petered out.

"Um. Yes." Nancy blinked and realized she had no concept of which direction she had taken out of the doctor's office parking lot. She now found herself headed straight toward Oak Bluffs, the opposite side of the island.

"I just have to pick up a bottle of wine, and then I'll be home."

Nancy stopped at the grocery store in Oak Bluffs and waited for a long moment, her hands still on the steering wheel. It felt intentional to go to the grocery in Oak Bluffs, as though her lack of directional abilities at that moment had all been purposeful. Once inside, she stopped to smile and greet several Oak Bluffs residents, all of whom she'd gotten to know well over the years.

"Lola! It's so wonderful to run into you." Nancy's heart fluttered at the sight of the beautiful late-thirties journalist Lola Sheridan. She had her hand over the top of a bottle of Cote de Rhone; a trendy pair of sunglasses were positioned on her head. "That article you wrote about the Lodge changed everything for us. I thought we were goners after that awful write-up from that horrible man."

Lola's smile widened. "To be honest, I took real pleasure in writing that. I can't imagine what kind of man would use someone like that to get to a story—especially one of the island girls. I hope Carmella wasn't too broken up about it? The last time I saw her, she mentioned something about Cody, and well—"

"It seems like she's finally realized she's in love with him."

"Beautiful. I love stories like that. When my sister got back together with her high school sweetheart, I thought my heart might just break in two," Lola admitted.

"And you? Any wedding bells for you and Tommy?"

Lola's eyelashes fluttered. "Tommy is a wild sailor boy with a chaotic heart. The fact that I got him to live with me is proof of something, I suppose. But a wedding ring? I don't know. Maybe neither of us is entirely open to the idea."

Nancy highly doubted that. No matter the wildness of a woman's heart, or the bohemian nature of her soul, Nancy felt sure that the union of marriage was a thing many, many women held dear. She knew this because she'd been a wild card for years, too— but Neal had given her the safety and love she had needed so much.

"Just keep me in the loop, dear," Nancy said with a secretive smile. "I would love to help you celebrate if it comes to that."

"If you want to tie him up at the altar, I'll see you there." Lola's laughter echoed through the grocery store. "But what brings you over here? This is the wrong neck of the woods for you."

"Ah, yes, it is. I had an appointment over here. I told Janine I would bring wine home."

"You're a good mother," Lola told her.

Nancy felt a strange stab of sorrow at the comment. After all, Lola's mother had died when Lola had been only eleven years old— a boating accident when an older man named Stan Ellis had turned off the lights of their boat and crashed. The fact that Anna Sheridan had been having an affair with Stan Ellis was often whispered about. It was the kind of gossip the island of Martha's Vineyard was built on.

"I'll see you around, Lola," Nancy said with a nod. "Always wonderful to see you."

When Nancy arrived home, she found Janine, Elsa, Carmella, and Mallory around the back porch table, halfway through the first bottle of wine already. She kissed them each on the cheek, sat down next to them, and forced her mind to follow their words down the wild trajectory of the day's stories. Still, every word was like water, and Nancy found them difficult to hold on to. When she peered back into her mind at the end of the night for some analysis of what had happened that evening, her memory was as empty as a dry well.

Chapter Three

Invasive.

It was the only appropriate word for the late morning and early afternoon that Thursday. Nancy forced her thoughts to hide away in a dark corner of her mind as she was poked and prodded and put through a series of official tests— each with a potentially deadly result. When the medical personnel explained the next step of a procedure, Nancy's lips curved into a smile as she set herself up for the next big performance. Why did she do that? Why did she want to be so agreeable as she faced this horrific future? She half imagined the medical staff thinking to themselves, *Wow, what a kind woman! This woman doesn't deserve whatever ailment we're testing her for— not in the slightest.*

Perhaps her kindness would mean she wouldn't have cancer. Maybe God would spare her and allow her an extra few years with the people she loved most.

This was a laughable thought. God didn't work like that. If he did, Neal would still be alive as he was the kindest and most endearing man on the planet. And assuredly, the medical staff who poked and prodded her had little thought for her personality. If she probed into their minds, she'd probably find thoughts about lunch or their children or their anxieties. She was just another patient passing through.

"Where have you been?" Janine popped out from the kitchen as Nancy entered the house. Janine wore a beautiful linen cream-colored suit, cinched tight at the waist with a dark belt. Her hair was angelic, as though lifted by a perpetual breeze.

"Hi, honey." Nancy's voice cracked the slightest bit. "I just had to meet a friend."

"You've been gone all day," Janine noted as her brow furrowed.

A strange silence passed between them. Nancy blinked, then forced a smile. "The girls must have left Woods Hole by now?"

Janine's healthy glow flowed off her again. "The ferry is headed straight for the island. We'd better go pick them up."

"Naw. Let's let them hitchhike," Nancy teased.

Janine and Nancy stepped into Janine's car and drove toward the ferry dock along the northern edge of the island. Throughout, Janine chattered both nervously and anxiously about the upcoming dinner that night held at the boutique hotel, The Hesson House. The dinner featured only close family and friends. The following evening was the rehearsal dinner before Saturday's main event: the marriage of Maggie to her dear love, Rex.

"I just can't believe she's getting married." Janine breathed the words as she turned off the engine a block away from the ferry dock. "I remember so clearly when she learned to ride a tricycle."

Nancy's throat tightened. Had she taught Janine how to ride a trike back in the day? She supposed that was the sort of toy she hadn't been able to afford. She had the strangest urge to ask Janine if she'd ever properly learned how to ride a bike but held it back. This weekend wasn't about her and her past regrets; it was about Maggie. It was about Janine. And Nancy was just grateful she was along for the ride.

Prior to that weekend, Maggie had shipped several items to Martha's Vineyard for the big event. Nancy had suspected this meant that Maggie and Alyssa wouldn't have so much luggage. However, the moment her Manhattan socialite granddaughters stepped into view from the ferry, Nancy recognized just how laughable that thought truly was. Maggie and Alyssa instructed three ferry employees on the suitcases they required. Behind them, two broad-shouldered twentysomething men— Rex, the groom, along with another young man, probably Alyssa's date, tiptoed along, careful not to say a word of ill will toward their girls' desire for a seemingly endless array of material possessions.

"I see they travel light," Nancy teased.

Janine flashed her mother a smile. "I tried my best not to spoil them."

"They're remarkable young women," Nancy assured her. "With insatiable fashion appetites."

The crowd of Vineyard guests swarmed the docks like bees. Nancy and Janine waded through to find their girls. Maggie flung her arms around her mother as the first of what would assuredly be many tears fled down her cheeks. Her fiancée looked on; his eyebrows were slightly

crooked. Alyssa leaned toward him and asked, "Are you
sure you want to marry this one? She's pretty dramatic."

Maggie swiped at her cheek and turned to give her
sister a rueful look. "Can you keep your sarcasm to a low
hum for the next few days? You know, I've waited for this
weekend my whole life."

Alyssa rolled her eyes. "Rex, you should have seen her
making me play dress-up back in the old days. I always
had to play the groom, and she was always the bride. It
wasn't fair."

An introduction was made to Alyssa's new boyfriend.

"This is Peter. Isn't he handsome?" Alyssa beamed as
Peter stretched a hand out to shake Janine's and Nancy's
hands.

"How did you two meet?" Nancy asked.

"Grandma, everyone meets everyone on the internet
these days," Alyssa informed her.

Nancy shrugged and made eye contact with Janine.
Their thought was the same: was romance completely
dead? But Peter's eyes glowed as he gazed at Alyssa; he
seemed to cherish her.

"Can't imagine what that would be like," Nancy said
as they headed back for Janine's car. The ferry workers
tugged the suitcases along behind them, following like
sheep. "Meeting someone from the internet sounds a bit
creepy. Were you scared?"

Alyssa arched an eyebrow toward her grandmother.
"Grandma, I don't know every story about your life, like
your wild hitchhiking days and your life all over the
world. I know you met Neal over in Bangkok, so I can
only imagine the kind of things you got yourself into."

Nancy's heart sped up slightly. This was the first time
she'd ever considered what her granddaughters thought of

her. Did they have some kind of strange respect for her, based on her experiences?

"What I mean is, I don't see how some stupid boy from the internet could scare you more than taking off to Bangkok by yourself," Alyssa said mischievously. "Sure. I met a handsome boy. But you took on the world. I think you're the brave one here."

Nancy's heart swelled with pride. As the ferry workers stacked suitcases into the back of Janine's car, Nancy drew her arms around her youngest grand-daughter and exhaled deeply.

If the tests came back badly—

If her life had to come to some kind of close—

She was so, so glad she had been allowed to know these women. She was so, so glad she'd been allowed to live as well as she had.

Rex and Peter lugged the suitcases back to the house and piled them across one side of the living area. Elsa padded down from upstairs and greeted everyone warmly.

"I have many bottles of wine chilling for you," she said as she greeted Maggie and Alyssa with light kisses on the cheek. "Mallory is upstairs with little Zach. They'll come down soon."

"Wonderful!" Alyssa cried.

It warmed Nancy to see Alyssa, Maggie, and Elsa's daughter, Mallory, together. Over the summer months, they had crafted a unique friendship. Despite the long, expansive hallways of Neal's mansion, Nancy sometimes still heard the three of them up late at night, tossing gossip from one end of their bedroom to the other as though they were still teenagers, rather than twenty-something-year-old women.

Nancy stepped into the kitchen with Elsa to gather wineglasses. Elsa flipped her long hair across her shoulders as she pulled open the refrigerator.

"Going to be a wild few days," she said as her eyes scanned the selection of rosé and white wines. "Haven't had a wedding in the family since yours and Dad's, I guess."

Nancy's heart cracked just the slightest at the memory. "Maggie looks so beautiful, doesn't she?"

Elsa's smile widened. "You're a sucker for your granddaughters, aren't you?" She placed several bottles of wine on the counter, then selected several fine cheeses and a container of black and green olives. "I'm so glad you got to meet them this year. What a whirlwind it's been! Imagine if Janine hadn't come back into your life? This wedding would have happened someplace else. You might have not even known about it at all."

Nancy splayed a hand on her chest across her heart at the thought. Her voice remained low. "I can't even tell you how grateful I am—for all of it."

"I know. I know you are." Elsa's smile widened as she began to draw open the packages of cheese and craft a charcuterie board. She then lowered her voice still more to add, "And what about Janine's ex-best friend?"

Nancy buzzed her lips. She drew open the antique cabinet toward the far end of the kitchen and began to collect wineglasses, slipping the stems through her fingers and hanging them from her hand.

"I've known Maxine as long as Janine has," Nancy breathed. "The girls were thicker than thieves. Always getting themselves into every type of trouble you could imagine. Once, when Maxine did something wrong at

25

school, Janine piped up to say she had done it too, just so they could have detention together."

"Wow, that's funny. Typical best friends," Elsa whispered.

"I know. It was the kind of friendship that should have extended across every decade. It was a powerful love between two girls, women. Something that I always thought was too magical to break. And then, as everyone knows…"

That moment, Janine stepped into the kitchen and brightly asked if Elsa needed any assistance. Her voice didn't skip a beat; probably, she hadn't heard the previous discussion. Nancy and Elsa caught one another's eye for the briefest moment; their looks were filled with relief that Janine hadn't listened in.

It wasn't like Janine needed reminding that her best friend had stolen her husband.

It wasn't like she needed reminding that they both would attend her daughter's wedding that weekend.

It was expected that they'd arrived on the island and would be at dinner this evening.

As Janine whipped past Nancy with two wineglasses in hand, Nancy placed a tender hand on Janine's elbow. Janine's manic energy swelled off her like waves onto a beach.

"Are you doing okay, Jan?"

Janine's eyes widened the slightest bit. "Yes, of course. My girls are here. What more could I want?"

Nancy nodded. "You'll tell us if you need us to do anything, right?"

"Of course."

This felt like a lie— one of the common lies women tell when they want to seem far stronger than they are.

The phrase "fake it till you make it" was assuredly invented by a woman.

Elsa placed the immaculate charcuterie boards at both ends of the porch table and silently helped Nancy pour white wine. Rex told a detailed tale of Maggie's recent bridezilla meltdown over the wedding appetizers, which had culminated in tears on the bathroom floor.

"I asked her, Maggie darling, do you think the world will end if we don't have stuffed mushrooms at the wedding? And she said point-blank, Rex, if we don't have stuffed mushrooms at the wedding, the world will end. Mark my words." Rex laughed uproariously at that as the others at the table joined in. Maggie's face turned beet-red.

"And I swear, that wedding planner, Charlotte Hamner, became a permanent fixture on our computer at the apartment," Rex continued as his smile widened. "Constantly telling Mags it would be all right. She had everything under control. And then every morning, like clockwork, Maggie would come up with another list of potential terrors and call Charlotte all over again."

Maggie laughed wildly. "I have a feeling Charlotte won't be too sad to see this wedding in her rearview mirror."

"You can't be the worst client she's ever had," Alyssa pointed out. "She did that crazy Ursula Pennington wedding last Thanksgiving. Charlotte is so brilliant that she managed to throw it together in just less than three weeks. I read about it in *People* magazine."

"Okay. Second worst, then," Rex insisted.

"Hey!" Maggie cried, her voice vibrant. Rex leaned over and kissed her gently, lovingly, on the cheek.

The immensity of their love brewed out from them

and seemed to brighten everything else. Nancy dropped her eyes to her glass of wine. Again, the fatigue returned, and her brain swam with fears and anxieties of what her test results would eventually reveal.

Let me stay here, her mind echoed. *Let me be with the women I love the most. Please.*

Chapter Four

The Hesson House was a newly opened boutique hotel just north of Edgartown. Olivia Hesson had been given the keys to the old-world mansion in the wake of her Great Aunt Marcia's death. In the months since, she and her boyfriend, Anthony, had worked tirelessly to craft a gloriously artistic space— one that upheld the minute detail of previous architectural and design areas while offering all the luxuries of the modern day. Charlotte Hamner had suggested The Hesson House's restaurant for the Thursday night dinner, and as they stepped through the foyer, they muttered agreements that this was the perfect locale.

Off to the right, a young woman sat at a grand piano and tapped her fingers across the keys delicately; her eyes were half-open as though with each chord and flick of her wrist, she dove deeper into a fictional, dream-like world.

Maggie's bridesmaids awaited them at a long table near the back. Also, two of Maggie and Alyssa's uncles from their father's side sat on the opposite end, along with a few cousins and their other grandfather and grandmother. Nancy nodded toward the grandmother, who, in truth, looked like a rueful and monstrous billionaire women— one of these women who had only ever gotten what she'd wanted in life and still refused to feel happiness.

For about the millionth time, Nancy cursed herself for not being around when Janine had gotten together with Jack Potter. Perhaps Nancy could have put a stop to it.

Not that Janine had been in any position to listen to what Nancy had to say. Nancy wouldn't have listened to that previous version of Nancy, either. She had been a near-constant train wreck— fun at parties and terrible at everything else.

Janine paused several feet from the table. Maggie bent to kiss her violent-looking grandmother on the cheek. There were muffled hello's until Maggie whipped around to hug her bridesmaids so hard they nearly popped.

"Where's Jack?" Janine whispered.

Nancy's heart hammered in her chest. She yanked her head around as though this would produce any sort of answer. Instead, she found only Carmella and Olivia Hesson in conversation near the piano. Carmella tossed her head beautifully and laughed at something Olivia said. Again, Nancy had this tremendous, ballooning feeling of loss; Carmella never laughed with her like that. Perhaps she never would.

"He should be here by now," Janine said, speaking again of Jack.

Maggie stepped behind her bridesmaids. Her eyes snapped up toward her mother and grandmother. Alyssa's nose pressed between Janine and Nancy's heads as she whispered, "Where the heck is Dad?"

Rex's parents arrived after that. There were introductions and hugs. Rex's father looked remarkably like him, and Elsa joked to Nancy that these Manhattan socialite people seemed almost built in a factory. Their perfection was top-notch.

"Shh," Nancy whispered into Elsa's ear. "Don't let them hear you say that. They're programmed to attack the minute someone guesses where they come from."

Elsa pretended to zip her lips closed and throw away the key. Across the table, Carmella eyed them and then dropped her gaze almost immediately. Jealousy was laced across her face, probably at Nancy and Elsa's powerful mother-daughter relationship. Something Nancy had no idea what to do about.

Maggie was seated two chairs away from Nancy, with Janine between them. Nancy thought she heard Maggie's whispered words as she curled against her mother. Janine then passed along the information to Nancy's ear.

"Apparently, Jack and Maxine aren't going to make it tonight or for the rehearsal tomorrow."

Nancy's eyes were wide as saucers. "You're kidding."

Janine looked on the verge of spitting fire. She drew her chair back and beckoned for Maggie to follow her. Alyssa and Nancy leaped from their chairs and hustled behind the two of them to a side hallway that led to the bathrooms. Maggie's eyes were rimmed red.

"I can't believe he's doing this," Alyssa blared suddenly. "It's like he wants to make some kind of stupid point."

"But what kind of point is he making? Just that he doesn't love me enough to be around for the most important events of my life. My wedding!" Maggie demanded.

"I don't know! I've never been the master of Jack

Potter. You know we fight like cats and dogs," Alyssa returned.

"Don't fight, girls. It gives him too much power over the situation," Janine insisted. She splayed her hands over her cheeks and stared into space.

"It's just that I told him over and over again not to bring her," Maggie said then. She crossed her arms so tightly over her chest that her elbows could have been used as swords. "And now, he's decided to punish me by not showing up at all."

"Is that something he would do?" Nancy asked softly, looking at each granddaughter.

Alyssa and Maggie both nodded their head unanimously. Janine eyed the ground, clearly panicked. Perhaps she didn't want Nancy to think badly of her, as she'd married this man and built a life with him.

People did crazy things with their lives. People acted wildly outside the bounds of reason. Nancy knew this better than most; it had been her MO for years. Nancy placed a hand over Janine's. More tears fled down Maggie's cheeks.

"I don't think we should worry about him tonight," Nancy interjected.

They ogled her, shock and confusion marring their faces.

"He didn't show up for this beautiful meal? That's his loss," Nancy affirmed. "He's going to look back at this moment when he's an old man and realize that he missed so, so many beautiful moments with his daughters, and he's going to regret it. I know because I regret every day I didn't know the two of you girls."

Alyssa wrapped an arm around Nancy's shoulder and leaned her head alongside hers.

"You're right." Maggie lifted her chin and set her jaw. "Let's not let him ruin this any more than he and Maxine already will."

"Gosh. I just can't stand it," Alyssa said pointedly.

"She was like our aunt," Maggie confessed to Nancy.

Janine turned back toward the table. Her hands shook slightly. "Let's go back to your guests. Your father's paying for this meal, isn't he? We should eat our weight in whatever we can get our hands on."

Janine and Maggie headed back toward the table. They walked side by side as their Louboutin heels clacked against the hardwood in unison. This left Alyssa and Nancy a bit behind. Alyssa hung her head so that her hair swung forward like curtains.

"What Maxine did to my mom makes me so fearful about everyone I've ever known," Alyssa said somberly.

"What do you mean?"

It was rare for these girls to open their hearts to their grandmother like this. To confide in anyone meant giving something of yourself, something you couldn't ever fully get back.

"Maxine and Mom loved each other like sisters. Their relationship was as close as me and Maggie's is, I swear. And then, Maxine just turned her back on Mom like that. It makes me wonder who you can ever really trust in your life, you know? Like, I tell myself that no matter what, I'm not alone. I have Maggie. I have Mom. And I now have you, Grandma."

Again, Nancy's heart swelled.

"It's one of the huge problems in life. You never know what will happen next or who will hurt you later. All you can do is love and love hard. The rest will fall into place."

Alyssa furrowed her brow. "I know you're right. I

know you are. And although I spent so long feeling terribly for Mom and what Maxine did to her, I look at her life now— at you, Elsa, Carmella, and the Lodge and, of course, her new Henry, whatever it is she's calling him these days—and I realize that in many ways, she's better than ever."

When Janine reached the table, she remained standing. Alyssa squeezed Nancy's hand, nodded toward her mother, and breathed, "At Maggie's engagement party, Mom wanted to make a speech so badly, but Dad wouldn't let her. He thought he was the only one worthy of making a speech, you know?"

"But now, it's your mom's time to take the floor," Nancy said.

"Exactly."

"Good evening, everyone." Janine's smile was electric. She looked fit for any movie screen. "I want to welcome you to a weekend I, for one, have looked forward to for many, many months. It's the wedding of my eldest daughter and, therefore, my first love, Maggie. Maggie, since you came into my world, you've been a boundless bundle of energy; you've made me laugh and cry and think bigger thoughts than I ever thought possible. And when you met Rex, I could see it in your eyes: you knew that everything had changed— and that nothing would ever return to what it had been before. And you knew you had to be brave enough to hold on to it with all your strength."

Janine lifted her glass of wine and spurred the others to do so, as well.

"Here's to the first of many toasts this weekend," Janine held up her glass. "To Maggie and Rex. May your happiness be lifelong. May you always turn to one another with love and compassion, and may you understand that life has no guidebook, no perfect next steps. The only real thing to have in this world is someone to laugh with. And as I've spent a good deal of time with both of you, I know you know how to do that."

"Cheers!" Everyone called out as they clinked their glasses and sipped.

Maggie beamed up at her mother and mouthed, "Thank you. I love you." Nancy turned toward Elsa, then wrapped her arms around her, overwhelmed with sorrow, tenderness, and love.

When their hug broke, Elsa reached across the table and collected Carmella's hand in hers. Carmella's eyes watered with tears, as well. She grabbed a bottle of wine, refilled her glass, and added more to Elsa's and Nancy's.

"I have a feeling it's going to be a waterworks of a weekend," Carmella said. She attempted to make eye contact with Nancy but soon fell away.

Their food arrived: crab legs, lobster bisque, and freshly-baked pieces of bread. Olivia Hesson arrived to greet them properly and congratulate the happy couple.

"The Hesson House only recently opened in July," she informed them. "You're only our third engagement celebration. We're so grateful to host you." She then snapped a photo of everyone at their table, explaining that she wanted to keep a record of these early days at The Hesson House.

"I never imagined that my dream would be to have a place like this," she said as she analyzed the photographs on her phone. "But seeing people like you gather here, all under one roof, to celebrate these particularly magical moments in your lives? It brings me to my knees."

That night, outside The Hesson House, Rex's various

groomsmen kidnapped him. They stuffed him into the back of a limousine and waved goodbye to Maggie, explaining they would take good care of him. Peter ran off with the boys as well, leaving Janine, Alyssa, Maggie, Carmella, Elsa, Nancy, and Mallory at the house yet again.

"That Peter guy of yours is handsome," Mallory said to Alyssa, her eyes wild.

Alyssa shrugged and weaved a curl through her fingers. "I just can't ever tell with these Manhattan boys. Does he like me? Or did he just want an expensive celebration on Martha's Vineyard? It's difficult to say."

"He likes you," Maggie affirmed. "Come on. He looks at you like you're a queen."

"Grandma. What do you think?" Alyssa turned earnest eyes toward Nancy. "You've probably dated your share of boys over the years."

Nancy's laughter rang out, as vibrant as music. "What makes you say that?"

"The life you've lived." Alyssa lifted a slender arm to grab a bottle of wine and refill her glass, then Nancy's, then Mallory's, and Maggie's. "All the men you must have known."

Nancy gave a half shrug. "I suppose so."

"Who was your favorite?" Maggie's question was earnest, bright.

"Well, of course, Neal Remington." Nancy gestured around the porch, to the open ocean below, along with the spacious house. "He gave me a life I'd never dreamed of and more love than I'd ever imagined."

"Yes. Yes. We know Neal was a saint," Maggie said, teasing her. "But we don't want to know about the saints."

"You know, Grandma, we want the good stuff."

Alyssa leaned forward, mischievous. "Give us your wild stories!"

Janine appeared in the doorway of the porch. "What are you guys trying to get your grandmother to do?"

Nancy felt her cheeks burn bright red. She heaved a sigh, turned her eyes toward the ceiling, and said, "Okay. Well, if you must know. There was this one man I met in Beijing. And he... well, he had the most beautiful motorcycle I've ever seen in my life."

"Whoa! Grandma!" Maggie and Alyssa cried in unison.

Janine clucked her tongue and said, "Don't give them any ideas, Mom."

"I think I have some ideas," Alyssa teased.

"Oh Lord have mercy," Janine joked. "Let's get through this wedding before you run off with a circus performer or something, okay?"

"I can't make any promises," Alyssa returned.

Chapter Five

The rehearsal and then the subsequent dinner went past in a flurry of wine drinking, wild conversation, and tear-soaked speeches— mostly from Janine and the groom's mother and father. They drowned in the language of, "What a beautiful couple," and, "Aren't they going to just have the most beautiful children?" and, "Rex treats her like a princess, doesn't he? And it's what she deserves."

All the while, whispers about Jack and Maxine's disappearing act fluttered through the growing crowd. "I can't believe he would do this to Maggie," was the consensus, while others suggested that the fact that he had broken up his marriage for Maxine was proof that he would stoop to the lowest of lows.

Throughout, Nancy was mesmerized by the way Janine handled herself. She walked like a queen with her shoulders back and her chin held high, and she greeted everyone warmly— even Jack's dear socialite friends— without embarrassment, as though the fact that Jack had abandoned their marriage and all they'd built together had hardly grazed her at all. Naturally, everyone knew this wasn't true; her very public breakdown had hit the tabloids hard. Still, that was what life was, wasn't it? Acceptance of the ways you'd faltered; belief in the ways you could build yourself up again.

Nancy had learned to believe in that. Janine seemed to do it naturally. She hadn't needed the many decades of screwups and failed relationships and running-around-the-world, running-from-herself mentality to learn, like Nancy. When Janine had been a toddler, a woman outside of their apartment at the time had grunted, cigarette dangling from her lips, as she'd told Nancy, Janine would teach her far more than Nancy taught her. At the time, a teenager herself, Nancy had only laughed at the idea.

Nancy sat in the gray light of the morning on the back porch with a green mug of coffee next to her. Far above the shoreline, a flock of Canadian geese crafted a perfect triangle formation and headed south. Nancy marveled at their ability to stick together, a constant team. She imagined herself, Janine, Maggie, Alyssa, Elsa, and even Carmella like those geese above: constantly headed forward through time, helping one another along.

"Morning." Janine stepped onto the porch in just a robe, her own mug of coffee in hand. Her dark hair cascaded beautifully across her shoulders, and her face remained clean and fresh, without the first layer of the day's coming makeup.

"How did you sleep?"

Janine gave a half-shrug. "I slept like I'm about to see Maxine for the first time since everything happened. I feel so refreshed." Her playful smile wasn't the least bit believable, but it was still gorgeous.

"Are the girls up yet?"

"I heard Mallory, Alyssa, and Maggie giggling about an hour ago," Janine said. "I can't imagine Maggie's finding it easy to sleep these days. Between the stress of the wedding and the excitement of binding herself to the love of her life forever."

"Yes, it's not easy to sleep through all of that," Nancy agreed with a laugh.

Janine dropped her head to the side so that her neck cracked.

"That sounds rough," Nancy said.

"Tense is all."

"Maybe we should have a yoga session," Nancy said suddenly. "All of us. The way we do at the Lodge, but right here."

It was decided. Janine and Nancy moved the porch table to the side to craft the perfect yoga space for all the women — Carmella, Elsa, Nancy, Janine, and Maggie, Mallory, and Alyssa. The girls agreed to the decision easily; it was the perfect antidote to the nervous energy that permeated the air.

Nancy stood like a ballerina before her tribe of women and lifted her arms joyously. A dull voice in the back of her mind reminded her that everything could very well go wrong, that one day soon, Dr. Morgan might report the horror that lurked within her veins. Perhaps soon, the earth wouldn't belong to her any longer. But in the wake of that, she wanted to remind her women of their inner strength. She wanted to give them everything she could.

"Remember. You are not your past," she echoed again

as they sat in a meditative pose. "But you can choose to mold your future however you please. Today, Maggie makes one of the biggest decisions of her life: one based on love and friendship and loyalty and hope. It is up to us, as the women who love her the most in the world, to uphold this decision and help her along the way— to ensure that she knows that for us, her happiness is paramount."

Elsa retreated into the kitchen to brew another pot of coffee when the yoga session was over. Carmella headed off to the Frosted Delights bakery to grab some turnovers and croissants for breakfast.

"Grab apple and raspberry. They're the absolute best," Maggie stated.

"Those are my favorites. Just the fuel we need," Nancy told her.

"We need it to talk to all those people you don't want to," Alyssa reminded her. "Like Dad's Aunt Stephanie."

Maggie shuddered. "She always smells like onions."

Janine burst into laughter. "Oh my, she really does. She was at my wedding a million years ago, and I remember recoiling from her smell."

"What is it?" Alyssa demanded. "Where does the smell come from? We've been to her apartment in Greenwich Village. It's stunning. Nothing smells like onions."

"It must just be her mean aura," Maggie joked. "She's spent all that time being judgmental of everyone around her, and it's manifested as an onion smell."

"If only it happened like that." Nancy smirked.

"If so, Maxine would smell like—" Alyssa began.

Janine arched an eyebrow as Alyssa snapped her lips shut tight. Silence brewed over them.

41

"Sorry," Alyssa said finally. "I didn't mean to bring her up."

Elsa appeared on the porch again with a fresh pot of coffee. Hurriedly, the table was put back in its rightful place, and they gathered around to wait for Carmella with breakfast. The other bridesmaids had begun to text Maggie excitedly about the approaching hours. Soon, they would meet at the Harbor View Hotel, in the room they had set aside for the long preparation. Makeup, hair, perfect fine-tuning of body and mind and spirit prior to the wedding ceremony and the subsequent photos— it would all happen in the magical space of that room. To Nancy's surprise, she'd also been invited to the room, along with Janine.

After they ate, it was time to pack up the cars. There was a frantic burst of energy. Maggie couldn't find her wedding shoes and burst into tears, only for Alyssa to find the box shoved to the side of the closet. Baby Zachery joined her crying a few seconds later; his face scrunched up and turned cherry-red as he wailed. Alyssa suggested that it was soon her turn to cry, then pretended to say, "Always a bridesmaid, never a bride!" Maggie just rolled her eyes and stepped into the passenger side of Janine's car. Janine's eyes found Nancy over the top of the vehicle.

"Are you ready for this?" Nancy asked with a funny smile.

"As ready as I'll ever be."

Nancy joined Alyssa in the back seat of Janine's car. Her dress had been packed up with the others in the larger vehicle, which Elsa agreed to drive over to the hotel. Maggie flicked through the radio stations, saying she needed "only the perfect music" for the last morning of her single life.

"She's so dramatic, isn't she?" Alyssa said to Nancy.

Nancy laughed. "I think it's good luck if you only listen to the things you love on your wedding day."

"See?" Maggie said pointedly to her sister. She then placed the cord into her phone and played what seemed to be some of her "favorite music," songs of singers from long-ago days that tugged at Nancy's heartstrings.

"Neal would have just loved that you liked these songs," Nancy said during a pause between the two of them.

"Really?" Maggie's eyes brightened in the rearview mirror. "Rex always teases me. He says I'm already an eighty-five-year-old lady."

"You look really good for eighty-five," Alyssa told her. "What's your secret?"

Several hotel staff members waited at the entrance to assist them with unloading the vehicles. One burly-looking thirty-something man tried to carry the wedding dress by himself, only to ask for assistance from another muscular guy after Maggie screeched, "Be careful with that!" Now, the two walked the dress delicately toward the door as though it was made of glass. Maggie watched them like a hawk.

The three bridesmaids awaited them in the preparation room, along with two women who had arrived to do their hair and makeup. One of the girls had brought a little stereo system and now played a bumping hip-hop track. She flung her arms around Maggie and said, "I wanted to remind you of our college days before you became a married woman."

"Oh gosh. This song? Remember when we..." Maggie trailed off.

"Danced on the bar on Santorini to this song? How could I forget?"

Nancy burst into laughter. "You girls. You're just like me."

Maggie's bridesmaid gawked at Nancy, whom she probably regarded as a "very old" woman. But Maggie took it in stride.

"My grandma had a crazy life," she told her friend. "She could probably teach us a thing or two about dancing on bars."

"My bar-dancing days are over," Nancy told them. "At the age of fifty-nine, I've finally grown up."

"She's lying to you about that," Janine told them brightly as she riffled through a bag of makeup. "Nancy Grimson-Remington will never grow up. Not really. It's against nature itself."

Nancy and Janine agreed to get their hair and makeup done simultaneously. They sat before the same mirror as two women sculpted their hair beautifully, then smeared creams, foundation, and perfect shades across their cheeks, eyelids, and lips.

"Maxine and I used to always get our hair and makeup done together before big functions," Janine said offhandedly, while the bride and her bridesmaids continued to gossip and giggle toward the far end of the room, near the stereo.

"Wow." Nancy could imagine the two of them in another era: Maxine and Janine, absolute beauties, making their way through the wealthy world of Manhattan socialites, even with their colossal secret: that they'd been born poor and grown up without anything, down in Brooklyn.

"But I'm glad it's you, now," Janine admitted. She tilted her head slightly to catch Nancy's eye in the mirror. "Really glad."

Nancy's heart swelled with gladness.

"The two of you look like sisters," one of the makeup artists recited then.

"I had her when I was sixteen," Nancy said. "You can imagine what a mess that was."

The makeup artist chuckled, and Janine joined in, her eyes light.

"Things always work out the way they're supposed to, don't they?" the makeup artist said as she fluttered a brush across Janine's cheek.

"That's what I have to believe," Nancy said.

"So you're the mother of the bride. And you're the grandmother," the artist continued.

"That's right."

"And how old were you when you married?" she asked Janine.

Janine's cheeks lost a good deal of their coloring. "I was very young, maybe too young to know what I was getting into."

"What did you think?" the artist asked Nancy. "About the wedding at the time?"

Nancy arched an eyebrow. Her throat tightened with sorrow. She hadn't been around for Janine's wedding. It was now one of her greatest regrets.

"I have always known Janine to have her head on straight," she said as brightly as she could. "She loves better than anyone I know. And she created two beautiful, intelligent women— people I can hardly believe are part of my lineage. How pleased I am that it all happened the way it did. I only wish I could go back and do it all over again."

Janine's eyes filled with tears. The makeup artist scolded her playfully.

"I don't want to redo all this makeup," she said. "So just try to hold in the waterworks until after pictures, okay?"

"I'll do my best," Janine offered. "But no promises."

Chapter Six

"You look remarkable."

The words echoed from behind Nancy as she focused on the mirror before them, where a fifty-nine-year-old woman in a dark blue dress with perfectly manicured nails and glorious, shiny hair peered back. The makeup and hair artist had performed a miracle. Nancy had never felt herself describe her form as "beautiful" before, yet here it was— this description.

Yet even as she stood, another wave of crashing fatigue came over her. Alyssa, who stood behind her in a pair of leggings and sweatshirt, placed her hand on her grandmother's shoulder to steady her.

"Whoa, Grandma. Just because I complimented you doesn't mean you can faint like some actress in a movie from the fifties," she teased. "But really, you should eat something! Those pastries will make all of us crash. I think we should order sandwiches."

"Not a bad idea," Janine agreed from the corner, where she had begun to fluff out Maggie's wedding dress.

"I'll get on that," Alyssa said dutifully. "I am the maid of honor, after all. I'd better take some responsibility."

Nancy winked as Alyssa walked away from them and lifted her phone to her ear. Again, the wave of fatigue pummeled against her heart. Nancy splayed a hand over her chest, closed her eyes, then counted to ten. During those ten seconds, she couldn't focus on the conversations that swirled around her; she could hardly hear Janine's voice as she hollered, "Mom? Mom!"

Nancy forced her eyes open to find her daughter before her. She blinked as the color returned to Janine's cheeks.

"Mom, are you okay?"

"She's just hungry," Alyssa said as she dropped her phone back into her purse. "But I'm on it."

Janine's eyebrows lowered. "You're sure it's just hunger?"

"I didn't sleep that well last night." Nancy waved her hand as though it didn't matter at all.

"Mom! What do you think of this?" Maggie hollered from the far end of the room, turning her face toward them to reveal a monstrous amount of makeup caked over her eyebrows, eyelids, and cheeks.

"Oops." Janine and Nancy both winced.

"One second." Janine eased back toward her daughter and the makeup artist, who'd apparently listened too intently to Maggie's description of "dramatic" makeup, "like a movie star."

Nancy might have laughed to herself. She felt the humor rise from her belly before it faltered and crashed. The fatigue was a constant cloud in the back of her skull. With everyone occupied, Nancy stepped into the hallway. She walked down toward the elaborately designed foyer, where she leaned heavily against the wall and forced herself to take deep breaths.

"If I'm going to leave this world, can I at least let this beautiful wedding day remain drama-free?" she begged the universe.

The woman at the reception rang the bell at the desk. Nancy opened her eyes to find her peering at her, curious.

"Can I get you anything, ma'am?"

"Some water would be wonderful if you have it."

The woman nodded, bent down, then reappeared with a fresh bottle of water chilled from a hidden fridge.

"Just put it on your room number," the woman said as she passed it over.

Nancy made a mental note to give cash to the woman later, as she wasn't a guest at the hotel. But in a moment, even that thought was gone. It was replaced with the glory of the sparkling drink in her hands, which now cascaded down her throat, giving her the sweet relief she needed. Maybe she hadn't been drinking enough water all these months? Perhaps that's all this illness was?

She padded away from the foyer and back toward where the wedding would be held. The weather had cooperated, and three-hundred and fifty chairs had been set up on either side of the outdoor aisle. The decoration was elaborate and autumnal, with plenty of deep ochres, belle époque tulips, and butterfly ranunculus to fit the beautiful season. Nancy stepped into the fresh air, directly in the space where her granddaughter would begin her march toward her beloved in just a few hours.

"Mom. I'm going to marry him."

It was a rogue memory. It assaulted Nancy's mind suddenly.

And the images came next.

Nancy gripped one of the chairs in the back row and closed her eyes tightly as the visions took hold of her.

* * *

"Mom. I will marry him. Just you wait."

This was Janine— a seven-year-old little girl, whom Nancy had just picked up from school, approximately forty-five minutes late, which wasn't so bad in Nancy-terms. After all, she had been hungover and had had to work a waitressing shift till three-thirty. What did the school know about "making ends meet"? It was either pick up her kid on time or put food on the table.

"Who are you talking about?" Nancy asked this of seven-year-old Janine. "Who are you going to marry?"

"Mom, I just told you. Gosh. Do you ever listen?"

Janine's haughty tone wasn't typical of a seven-year-old. Nancy stopped short on the sidewalk and glared at her daughter. "Excuse me. What did you just say to me? Do you want to get grounded again?"

Janine's nostrils flared. Nancy couldn't help but notice how much the girl looked like herself at that age. She only had a few photographs, but there in front of her, her face was illustrated in a different era.

"You just never listen!" Janine yelled, then cast herself forward, ripping down the sidewalk.

"Get back here!" Nancy didn't have time for anything like this. She burst through the crowd as the colossal weight of her hangover barreled back down upon her. "Janine! Where are you going!"

Janine whisked from sight. Nancy continued to run until her thighs screamed. When her breath ran out, she stopped at the corner and cried toward the sky above. Janine had escaped her, and in the core of Nancy's heart, she knew that Janine would probably be better in this world without her.

Nancy just wasn't equipped to care for her. She wasn't equipped to show her the love she so deserved. She just couldn't find it within herself. She was too damaged.

Suddenly, there was a tug on her elbow. Nancy whipped around to find Janine in the midst of a giggle. It seemed like she had watched her mother tear through the crowd ahead of her, and she had poised somewhere behind, lying in wait until Nancy fully broke down. Nancy wanted to scream, but instead, she dropped down on one knee, wrapped her arms around her daughter, and shook with her sobs. This scared little Janine all the more.

"Mom, it's okay! It's okay!"

But it wasn't. Nancy knew it wasn't. She leaned back as her cheeks caught the chill of the autumn wind. When was the last time Nancy even knew what day of the week it was? Why was her life such a mess?

"Who are you going to marry?" she finally whispered, her voice cracking. "Please tell me. I want to know everything about you."

Nancy blinked the memory away as she pressed her hand against the door at the wedding venue in Edgartown, even as her mind continued to sift through more memories. Images clouded her. With every step, she saw more: the dirty pillow on the bed in the apartment they'd lived in when Janine had been a baby; the fact that they had gone months without seeing the bottom of the sink, as she'd been too depressed to do all the dishes; the fact that she'd had a steady stream of boyfriends during Janine's youth, men who'd been scared of the idea of children. Nancy had felt resentment toward her daughter during those years; she had blamed her for her loneliness.

How awful.

Why was she stewing in these memories now?

A hot flash came over her. Nancy stood near the closet— a dark, shadowy, empty closet. Without thinking, she walked inside and closed the door quickly. She then placed her forehead against the cool plaster and exhaled as much air as she could.

Pull yourself together, Nancy. Come on. Do it for Janine's sake. Do it for Maggie's sake. Do it for the sake of new memories, which could very well blot out the old.

But they came back to her, fast and heavy. The closet's darkness made her fall into them without pause, as the rest of the outside world now felt like a faraway idea.

The letter—the letter she'd received from Janine all those years ago. It had explained in direct detail that Janine didn't need her mother and would never again. The letter had explained her newfound love for Jack Potter. Finally, Janine found someone to protect her, care for her, and "love her the way she deserved to be loved."

How Nancy had cried after she'd received that letter. The immensity of her love for her daughter had followed her around like a shadow over the years; it had taunted her, told her continually, especially on dark nights, that she wasn't enough for anyone, least of all the creature she'd created. The news that Janine had found happiness with someone had hit her hard.

And she'd so yearned to be a member of the crowd at that wedding. As Jack was a part of the Manhattan elite, everyone who was everyone had attended the wedding—except, of course, the mother of the bride. Nancy had dreamed about that day perhaps once a month since. Mothers were meant to be calm, powerful sources of energy on their daughter's wedding day. Mothers were meant to be the way Janine was, just now, for Maggie. Nobody had taken Janine aside to give her advice about love and marriage. "I was so lucky to be your mother. I'm still so lucky to be your mother." Nancy should have been there.

Regrets.

They shimmered through the back of her skull.

Now, if the test results came back with bad news? Now, if her life was on the brink of collapse? What did any of that mean?

She'd wasted so much time.

Outside the door was the sudden slam of another door, then the hiss of volatile words. Nancy furrowed her brow as her focus shifted.

The voices were hushed but laced with anger. A male and a female, probably a couple, lurked just beyond the closet door. Nancy and Neal had hardly gotten into arguments, but Nancy had had her share of them over the years with other partners, and the sounds of this one were triggering. She pressed her hands on the cool wall before her and inhaled then exhaled, as the fight escalated just outside of where she stood.

"I don't know why you thought that was appropriate," the man blared, louder now than before, as though he had lost all sense of where they were.

He probably didn't suspect that an older woman lurked in the closet beside him. It wasn't something anyone would expect. Nancy prayed that soon, they would take their argument elsewhere so that she could slip out and run back to her daughter and granddaughters unnoticed.

But it seemed likely that they wouldn't leave away any time soon.

"Jack. Can you find it within yourself to calm down?"

The woman's voice had the slightest French accent to it. Nancy's heart dropped into the pit of her belly.

It was Jack and Maxine. Jack and Maxine were in a heated argument just outside her door. Nervousness and goose bumps on her skin stood on end as she contemplated what to do next. These people were her daughter's enemies, and for this reason, Nancy felt poised to attack. She had missed most of her daughter's life. But now, she planned to stand up for her daughter any way she could. Maybe she was on her way out of this world, and if so, she would make this final mark before she left it.

She would be heard.

Chapter Seven

"I can't believe you wore that." Jack's words were harsh, dark, and brooding. From her many years of working with emotionally injured people, Nancy knew that these were the words of an arrogant, manipulative man-child.

"And what did you expect me to wear? Hmm? Why don't you give me a list of expectations, Jack, so I can always do as you ask?"

Maxine was just as snarky as she'd always been. Nancy suppressed a smile and reminded herself that Maxine was the enemy now, too. Still, she had to relish that the two of them didn't seem to get along.

Plus, it burdened her to realize just how cruel this man could be. Her Janine had spent so many years with him. This was the father of her beautiful granddaughters! There was no way to know what kind of cruel words he selected for Maggie and Alyssa. Assuredly, he had poisoned their mind with his horrific arrogant opinions in the past. Nancy's hands clenched into fists at the thought.

"I would have assumed you knew better, Maxine. Although it's funny, what's assumed. You've done a perfectly wonderful job showing me just how much credit I gave you and just how much you don't live up to that standard," Jack hissed, his voice laced with disgust.

"You bastard," Maxine returned.

"You slut."

Nancy couldn't stop herself. The words were so grotesque; she shoved herself through the closet door and surprised the pair of them, who turned their bright eyes to stare at Nancy in shock. Nancy remained in the doorway and inspected them for a moment.

Maxine wore a silver dress, which surged over her breasts and hugged her curves. The large slit up the side of her thigh hovered dangerously close to her hipbone. Her hair curled beautifully across her shoulders, and her makeup made her look like a smoldering temptress. Perhaps she had put herself together this way as a final show-off for Janine? It was some kind of statement, whatever it was.

Jack looked incredibly handsome. In some respects, he had the good luck of having gotten better looking over the years, with his hair sprinkled with salt-and-pepper strands, his shoulders broad, and his chin chiseled. You could practically smell the wealth on him in the suit he was wearing. It went along with the arrogance like a perfume.

Nancy turned her eyes toward her son-in-law, flared her nostrils, and said, "I don't care who you are. You don't speak to women that way—ever!"

Maxine's mouth opened in continued shock. Under her breath, she whispered, "Nancy. Is that you?"

Silence stewed between them. Jack's face took on

many different emotions. His shock transformed into rage, which eventually turned toward an ominous arrogance that frightened Nancy greatly.

Why had Janine married this man? Nancy supposed she had given her no reason to trust her instincts. After all, her mother had abandoned her; they'd never had two pennies to rub together. The world had been extremely cruel and dark, and Jack had lent her a helping hand—and his empire along with it.

"Nancy Grimson, I presume?" Jack said then. His smile was cutting.

"Remington, actually." Nancy stepped toward him and slammed the door closed behind her.

"It's wonderful to meet you," Jack continued. "I've heard so much over the years."

"I can't say it's a pleasure to meet you," Nancy returned.

"Ah, honesty. How refreshing. Maxine, don't you think it's refreshing?"

Nancy turned her eyes toward Maxine. Within her gaze, she found that same young, naive girl from thirty years ago. A girl who'd taken up residence at her kitchen table nearly every evening as she and Janine had gossiped and eaten snacks. Where had the time gone?

"I didn't know you and Janine had — um." Maxine pressed her lips together. She'd gone over the line, and she knew it.

"Oh, yes. Janine and I have patched things up," Nancy finished her sentence.

"How marvelous," Jack said flippantly. "It's good that she caught you between benders, though, isn't it? Oh, Nancy Grimson-Remington. You're a wild one, aren't you? Quite famous. The list is long, like when you didn't come home for three days when Janine was fourteen? And she found you in the middle of a wild rage on the sidewalk?"

Nancy's heart slammed against her rib cage. Jack would use any ammunition he had against her. No doubt, he had a lot. And it's not like she could blame Janine for telling him these stories. They had been life partners; she'd thought she could trust him.

She again thought back to what Alyssa had said about not trusting anyone in this world. Anyone could double-cross you at any time.

"That's none of your business anymore, is it, Jack?" Nancy told him. Her voice wavered dangerously.

"Perhaps not, but I suppose the better question is, why do you involve yourself in my business? Stalking me? Hovering in little closets, waiting to attack?" He beamed at her, pleased with himself.

Anger marred Nancy's beautiful face as she held his glare. She wouldn't back down to this awful creature that called himself a man. He might have been told stories of her past, but that was in the past, and this was the future. She'd been stewing in her own trashy memories of how crappy of a mother she'd been to Janine, so be damned if she would allow Jack Potter to add to her misery. She took one step closer to Jack and snarled, "Why would I ever stalk a little man like you? One of such unimportance to this family. I swear if you make a scene at this wedding, you will regret it, Jack." At that, she stepped around him and stormed out of the room, slamming the door behind her. She ran down the corridor, turned a corner, then leaned against the wall, trying to catch her breath as she blinked her tears away.

She'd felt awful about her past. She'd ruined her

daughter's life — and she'd also ruined her own. She felt herself spiraling, falling deeper and deeper into a dark hole, an abyss she'd always known awaited her yet had been allowed to shove to the side in the previous decade since she'd met Neal.

She couldn't outrun it forever. It was here, and it was hungry for her.

"Nancy?" The voice rang out from the side of the hallway. In a moment, a tender hand appeared on Nancy's back.

Nancy turned her head slowly and blinked several times again until the angelic face of Elsa appeared before her.

"Nancy, are you all right?"

Nancy swallowed the lump in her throat.

"Carmella, can you help me lift her?" Elsa asked.

Nancy had been so far away that she hadn't realized Carmella was there. Another pair of hands appeared on her shoulder and slowly, softly helped her gain her balance. Nancy felt like a toddler, learning to walk for the first time. Every step seemed so unsure.

Before she knew it, they had positioned her on a bench near the hotel lobby. Elsa remained alongside her, an arm around her shoulder, while Carmella retreated to find water and a snack.

"Nancy, are you all right?" Elsa whispered again.

"I don't know how to answer that." Slowly, the world seemed to draw itself forward again. Nancy's thoughts seemed more confident. Her breaths were deeper, and her eyes were more focused.

"Did something happen?"

Nancy swallowed again. "I ran into the father of the bride, Jack Potter. What a horrible man."

Elsa furrowed her brow. "Wow. So he arrived on time, then."

"Apparently so."

Carmella returned with a granola bar and a bottle of water. Nancy opened the wrapper around the granola bar and bit down softly. The chocolate melted across her tongue.

"Weddings are always a lot to handle," Carmella said, as though she didn't know what else to say.

"Lots of stress for everyone involved," Elsa agreed. "I remember my wedding. I nearly collapsed from all the anxiety."

"You kept forgetting to eat," Carmella told her. "I had to chase you down with a sandwich. And then, you got mad at me and told me I didn't want you to look your best for your pictures."

Elsa laughed. The laughter was so nourishing in Nancy's ears. Her lips curved upward into a smile.

"You girls shouldn't sit here with me while I fall apart," Nancy said. "You should be with Bruce and Cody."

"Don't be silly. Bruce and Cody can handle themselves," Elsa affirmed. "We left them out by the pre-wedding open bar, mid-way through the most boring conversation ever about sports."

"Isn't that every conversation about sports?" Nancy asked. Laughter bubbled up from her stomach as her strength grew.

"I'm just glad we can sit them together and let them hash whatever sport-lingo out," Carmella smiled, tucking a strand of hair behind her ear. "Cody and I can talk about almost anything, but I have to draw the line somewhere."

Elsa's grin widened. Nancy placed her head on her stepdaughter's shoulder and exhaled deeply.

"Come on, Nancy. You'd tell us if there was something really wrong, wouldn't you?" Elsa asked.

Nancy knew, of course, that she wouldn't. Still, she nodded another lie. Carmella's eyes dropped toward the floor. There was still such a boundary between the two of them. How could Nancy possibly penetrate it?

"I just didn't sleep well last night. And then, when I encountered Jack and Maxine, I fell apart."

"I think we should kick those monsters off the island," Elsa affirmed. "I feel morally opposed to the idea of Jack and Maxine, especially now that I've fallen for Janine."

"But at least she's out of that marriage," Carmella pointed out. "This might be one of the last days we have to interact with him."

"Today and Alyssa's wedding, that is," Elsa corrected.

It warmed Nancy's heart to think of her stepdaughters, including Alyssa's wedding in the grand scheme of their lives together. Their love had extended out easily.

"I had better get back to the girls," Nancy told them as she tried to smooth out some minor creases in her dress.

Carmella and Elsa exchanged glances.

"Let's fix up your makeup first," Elsa suggested. "I have some stuff in my purse."

"Is it that bad?" Nancy thought back to the tears, the sweat, and the dread that had permeated everything else in that closet.

"No, of course not," Elsa replied with assurance. "But I don't want Janine to worry. She has enough on her plate."

Nancy followed after Elsa and Carmella. They

stepped into the ladies' room, where she took stock of her reflection, which looked like a ritzy-looking raccoon. Elsa fixed up Nancy's makeup with a gentle hand, then sent her back on her way.

"See you at the reception," Elsa flashed her a smile. "You look beautiful."

"Thank you for your help," Nancy told her. "I thought I lost my mind there for a minute."

"If you ever lose your mind, we can help you get it back," Elsa affirmed. "We know what it's like to misplace it. Don't we, Carm?"

Carmella gave Nancy a genuine smile, one of warmth, tenderness, and understanding. Nancy's heart ballooned with love.

Chapter Eight

Maggie looked immaculate, as though she had stepped from the world of old-time movie stars, ritzy nostalgia, and glorious dreams. She stood near the glass door, mere feet away from where the aisle began, and watched as the guests milled in from the outside parking lot. Blue skies remained stretched overhead, and there was still a tinge of summer to the air, which added a sense of excitement and beauty to this day, one of the most important of her life.

Nancy and Janine stepped up alongside her. Alyssa joined on Nancy's other side. There was the flash of a camera just behind them. This iconic photograph was three generations of women, all facing the future, stronger together than apart. Nancy made a mental note to place this photograph in her house. She wanted to remain in this moment as long as she could.

Janine dropped her hand over her mother's and squeezed it gently. Nancy grabbed Alyssa's on the other side, and the four of them stood, linked until Charlotte Hamner arrived to announce it was almost time to walk down the aisle. Her cheeks flushed crimson with excitement and stress. Maggie beamed at her and thanked her for all she'd done.

"I'm sorry if I was kind of a bridezilla," she murmured as she adjusted her veil with a nervous hand.

Charlotte laughed. "You weren't. Not in the slightest. Everything has fallen into place. It's up to you to just enjoy every little bit about this day. You can't get it back. Remember, I've got everything taken care of behind the scenes."

Maggie nodded firmly. Charlotte pressed her earpiece and spoke to someone on the other end. "It's nearly go time." The air sizzled with expectation.

"Where's Jack?" Alyssa asked then. "He texted that he was here a few hours ago."

Maggie shrugged. "If he doesn't make it, I guess Mom can just walk me down the aisle. It's what I want, anyway."

Alyssa looked at Janine and then Maggie. "I agree. I don't think he deserves this moment."

"Well, let's wait a few more moments and see," Maggie quipped.

Janine's eyes dropped toward the ground. Awkwardness seemed the name of the game. How Nancy wished she could eliminate the concept of Jack Potter from the world, but this was his daughter, and this was a day of celebration for him, too. Regardless, the thought made Nancy set her jaw.

Henry appeared in the doorway. He was dressed wonderfully in an expensive suit, his hair slightly ruffled, and his skin still tanned from his many afternoons on the sailboat over the summer months. Nancy had gone with Henry and Janine several times since they had begun their fledgling relationship. Henry now beamed at Janine with immense love in his eyes.

"I wanted to wish you all good luck," he beamed at them all.

"We're going to need it," Janine told him, her smile widening. "Who knows what might happen. We could trip going down the aisle."

"Mom! Don't jinx us," Maggie hissed.

Janine stepped forward and kissed Henry's cheek, one that left the slightest smear of lipstick.

"Save me a dance later?"

"I'll be the awkward one in the corner, waiting for my turn with you," Henry said.

Alyssa stepped forward. "Come on, you two. Don't make us throw up."

Henry gestured toward the growing crowd. "I'd better grab myself a seat, I guess. This is the Martha's Vineyard event of the century."

"Something like that," Maggie replied with a nervous laugh.

Henry stepped out and then walked to one of the bride-side rows. Janine continued to grin, her eyes cast downward as though she swam through her own dreamland.

"Mom's in love," Maggie sang. "Look at her. She's like a schoolgirl."

"Oh, you quit it." Janine swatted her daughter's arm playfully.

Suddenly, Jack Potter appeared in the doorway. His cheeks tinged red as though he'd already had too much to drink. His eyes scanned the group— the bridesmaids alongside Janine and Nancy—until he found the bride herself.

"There she is— my Maggie."

Nancy was surprised at how warm his words sounded. He stepped toward her, wrapping his firm arms around her as though his entire life mission was to protect her from the evils of the world. Nancy's heart thudded strangely. People were complicated. People held universes within their small brains. On the one hand, this man was a monster, but on the flipside, he loved his daughter very much.

When Jack finally stepped back, his eyes were rimmed red with tears. "I can't believe you're getting married today, Mags. I still remember when you took your first step."

He glanced right-ward toward Janine. Janine held his gaze for a moment before she dropped all eye contact. Guaranteed, they could feel the old memories, the immensity of their story together. Still, they could also feel the enormity of the pain and destruction that took place between them, especially for Janine.

"But Rex is a great guy," Jack continued. "One of the best that a father could ask for. I mean, I still remember that idiot you dated in high school."

"Dad..." Maggie said as her smile widened.

"It's true. He was a clown." Janine nodded in agreement.

"Right?" Jack's laughter was infectious.

Nancy could feel it, then. It seemed obvious why Janine had fallen head-over-heels for this man. He was endlessly charming when he wanted to be. In a weird way, she was pleased that he had decided to draw out this "charm" right then, minutes before his daughter walked down the aisle. These were precious memories, despite their imperfections. Maybe their imperfections made them more precious. It was difficult to say.

Jack then turned toward Alyssa, whose expression was stern and shadowed. Maggie was the more carefree one of the sister-duo; Alyssa held grudges. Nancy kind of liked this about Alyssa. It reminded her of herself.

"Alyssa," Jack said in greeting.

"Jack," Alyssa returned.

"Come on, honey. Don't be this way," Jack told her.

"Be what way, Jack?" Alyssa returned.

Jack turned his attention back toward Maggie. "You ready to take this big leap?"

Maggie nodded. "Ready as I'll ever be."

Charlotte Hamner reappeared to tell them it was nearly time to walk down the aisle. Nancy headed out to her reserved chair, located on the right-hand side in the front row, mere feet from where Maggie and Rex would pledge their lives to one another. Beside her, Elsa, Bruce, Carmella, and Cody all sat serenely. Elsa gripped Nancy's hand and squeezed it.

"Are you feeling better?" she asked. "You look beautiful."

Nancy nodded. Off to the right, the string quintet swelled into the first song, which would bring the bridesmaids down the aisle. Nancy's heart fluttered like a rabbit's. Far down the row and three back, she spotted Maxine, who stared straight ahead with a stony expression. Nancy might have paid good money to ask Maxine what she thought of all this. For years, she'd been something of an aunt to Maggie and Alyssa. Now, the girls hated her more than the devil himself.

The bridesmaids arrived one by one, lining up on one

side of the aisle, making space for the groomsmen on the other side. Rex stood center-stage, his hands folded over his waist as he awaited his bride. His eyes stirred with fear and longing. Despite his late-twenties age, he looked so youthful to Nancy. It was remarkable that young people seemed to have so much of an idea of what they wanted in the world. It had taken Nancy decades to figure out what she'd wanted. And even then, it had felt like a leap into the ether.

There was no way to ever know if the decisions you made were correct.

The quintet changed the song to the wedding march. It was time for Maggie to make her dramatic journey down the aisle. Everyone stood to turn back. Janine finished her route down the aisle, then stepped in beside Nancy, where a final seat remained on her left. Janine's eyes were rimmed with tears.

"I don't know if I can hold it together," she told Nancy before she turned back to fully take in the sight of her soon-to-be ex-husband walking her darling daughter down the aisle.

Maggie walked with confidence, like a queen. After all, she was Manhattan royalty and had been trained to be looked at and appreciated in all her glory since she'd been a young girl. Even still, the effect was mesmerizing. Several paparazzi had been allowed to attend the wedding and now flashed their cameras to take in full view of Maggie and her ornate, vintage wedding dress. Beside her, Jack Potter beamed, showing off his pride and joy, his daughter on the brink of marrying into another wealthy New York City elite family.

Still, regardless of the status of the families, there was immense love within this union. Looking into Rex's eyes, you found an endless promise of commitment, respect, and love. Nancy's heart fluttered with the memory of Neal's eyes on their wedding day. His had been the same.

She felt it in her bones. Maggie had found her life partner— not the sort of man who would leave her for her best friend after twenty years of marriage. At least, Nancy prayed that was so.

Jack and Maggie appeared at the front of the aisle. He kissed her cheek and stepped off to the side, where he grabbed a chair toward the end of the row. Nancy noticed that he didn't bother to sit next to Maxine. Perhaps their fight hadn't been resolved.

Silence filled the air as the pastor stepped forward to begin the service. Rex took Maggie's hands in his and wagged his eyebrows playfully. Maggie seemed to suppress a giggle. Nancy prayed that they would always share such a sense of humor; she prayed that they would always find a way toward laughter, even in the darkest times.

A tear rolled down Janine's cheek. She snapped a finger up to catch it. Nancy leaned over and whispered into her ear.

"She looks beautiful. And so, so happy."

Janine nodded. The look she gave Nancy made Nancy's heart nearly burst.

"I know I've already had to say goodbye to her," Janine breathed. "But this just feels so final."

"You know these girls can't get enough of you," Nancy told her. "They're always knocking on my door, begging for more time."

"And I hope it's always like that," Janine whispered. "I never want them to be far away from me. The way we were."

Nancy's tears now threatened to fall. She'd swum

through countless stories of resentment, fear, and sorrow only that afternoon. Now, she had to focus on her inner strength, if only for Janine's sake.

"We have a lot of love to pass around, Janine," she whispered. "This is only the beginning."

Maggie and Rex had both written their vows; much like Nancy and Neal had done all those years before. Nancy and Janine held hands as they listened.

"Rex, from the moment I met you, I felt at home in your arms," Maggie said tenderly. "I knew you would always be there to guide me and make me laugh, to show me how silly I can sometimes be, and to remind me that there is always something good around the corner if you only have the optimism to look for it."

Optimism! What a strange concept that had been before Neal had come around. Even after so many decades of darkness, Neal had taught Nancy how to search for it.

"I love you," Maggie breathed, locking eyes with him. "And I pledge to honor that love every single day of the rest of my life."

Nancy's heart felt squeezed. Tears welled in her eyes and then rolled down her cheek. She had returned to her previous state as the messy, fifty-nine-year-old raccoon-eyed lady. But just then, she didn't care. Maggie pressed her lips against her groom and fell into marriage, just like that. If she had the optimism to hope for this beautiful future with Rex, then Nancy had the optimism to keep living— as long as her body allowed it.

Chapter Nine

"Alyssa! Can you please concentrate?" Maggie blared from inside the bathroom stall, where the two sisters had ducked out for Maggie's post-photograph bathroom break. Nancy and Janine waited near the sinks and exchanged glances as a large white dress fluffed near the floor. "If you let me fall into this toilet on my wedding day, so help me, God."

"Chill out, Mags," Alyssa told her. "Or else I'll push you into the toilet myself."

"Girls? Do I have to come in there?" Janine threatened as she suppressed a laugh.

"Mom! Tell Alyssa to stop messing around. This is serious."

Janine arched an eyebrow toward Nancy and whispered, "This is exactly how they were as kids. Perfect children until they get tired and hungry."

"I'm starving!" Alyssa hollered from within the stall. "Can you go grab me one of those appetizers?"

Janine laughed and turned back to face the mirror. She leaned forward and drew a line across her lip with her perfectly manicured nails. As Alyssa and Maggie quieted down, Nancy joined her daughter at the sink and re-applied some eye shadow, just for something to do.

"It was a beautiful ceremony," she told Janine. "It really was."

"So far, so good. No real drama yet," Janine murmured.

Nancy burned to ask her daughter what had happened when she'd seen Maxine. Had they had any contact yet? Janine heaved a sigh and righted her shoulders.

"I'd better go make the rounds and find Henry. He's fine on his own, but I feel bad leaving him out there among the wolves. Are you coming?"

"I'll join you in a bit," Nancy told her.

Maggie and Alyssa scrambled from the bathroom, bursting out from the stall as though they'd been physically stuffed inside. Alyssa made a final adjustment to Maggie's gown. Maggie investigated her makeup and then practiced her smile in the mirror.

"You're a freak," Alyssa said to Maggie's reflection.

"Easy for you to say. All eyes are on me tonight," Maggie told her. "I have to look my best."

"You look simply magnificent," Nancy told Maggie.

"You have to say that, Grandma," Maggie said. "Or they'd revoke your grandmother card."

Nancy chuckled as Alyssa smeared some blush across her cheek.

"Grandma, I wish you had a date out there," Alyssa confessed with a sad smile.

"Maybe you could save me a dance?" Nancy teased.

Alyssa nodded. "It would be my honor."

The girls disappeared after that. Nancy walked into

the stall and exhaled long and slow, trying to have full control over her thoughts again. She felt the fatigue curl around the back of her skull, a constant reminder that all was not so well. As she perched at the edge of the toilet seat, three women walked in with the click of their high heels echoing throughout the room. They paraded around the sink and mirror, already gossiping.

"You saw what Maxine was wearing, didn't you?" one of the women said.

"She looks — hmm — like she's trying to prove something," another woman affirmed.

"You think? All that cleavage and that cut up the leg?" Her voice was heavy with sarcasm.

"I spotted Janine and Maxine just a few feet away from one another while the photographs were being taken," another said. "You could feel the air shift. I expected an earthquake to happen."

"Poor Janine. Everyone at the wedding can only talk about one thing. Her divorce and her breakup from Maxine."

"Well, Maxine and Janine were thicker than thieves. And they grew up poor, which, apparently, binds people together."

"Not that you would know that," another woman chimed in, just as she let out a high-pitched, screeching laugh.

"Do you think Maxine regrets it?"

"What? Haven't we all talked about hooking up with Jack Potter at one time or another?"

"I'm happily married, thank you very much," another pointed out.

"As if any of us are happily married."

"Oh, you're cruel, Samantha."

Nancy's heart dropped into the pit of her gut. One by one, the women either walked into other stalls or headed back into the bubbling chaos of the reception. Nancy stepped out, washed her hands, then headed into the hallway.

Happiness and lifelong commitment— what did any of it mean? And was a wedding between Maggie and Rex the place for such an awful intrusive conversation about divorce and betrayal? Nancy stepped off toward the drink table and ordered a vodka tonic, which she drank slowly through a straw, eyeing the rest of the crowd. The string quintet from earlier played light tunes; the string sounds swelled through the air as they eased their bows this way, then that.

Maxine stood about fifteen feet to Nancy's right. She clutched what looked to be a martini and stared straight ahead. She had that perpetually cool, French regal feel to her even there at her ex-best friend's daughter's wedding. She should be studied by science. How could a woman perform such a cruel action?

Janine burst out from the far end of the crowd, no more than five feet from Maxine. The two women locked eyes. Janine faltered; her heel dropped to the side, and her knee fell. Maxine leaped forward and grabbed her elbow as the crowd around them gasped. Nancy placed her vodka tonic off to the side and hustled forward to help. Meanwhile, Janine's eyes found Maxine's as Maxine righted her. Gossip swirled instantly.

"Did she push her?" one woman asked as Nancy rushed past.

"I wouldn't put it past her."

"Catfight!"

Everyone would have loved it if that rumor had been

true. All that had happened was Janine tripping in her overly high, overly expensive heels and another woman helping her to her feet. It was simple: a generous act between two humans.

"Jan. Are you okay, honey?" Nancy appeared beside her daughter as Maxine's arm dropped to her side.

Janine adjusted her dress. Her eyes remained on Maxine's. The number of words unsaid between these two women could have filled a dictionary.

"I'm fine," Janine finally blurted out.

Maxine sniffed. She offered no smile. "Nancy. Janine," she finally said. "Good to see you both together again."

Janine's eyes squinted, indicating her uneasiness. She shifted her weight. "I've lived here on Martha's Vineyard with Mom since June."

Nancy was surprised Janine gave Maxine any of this information. Perhaps it came from some kind of habit. Maybe the moment Janine saw her lifelong best friend, she wanted to blurt out all the inner-aching of her soul. After all, Janine had said that one of the hardest things about losing Maxine had been that she couldn't discuss her divorce with her dearest friend. "She was taken from me, and she did the taking," Janine had said.

"I'm so glad you found one another again," Maxine offered.

Nancy placed her hand around Janine's elbow and tugged tenderly. Janine seemed regretful about leaving. The cocktail hour would soon be finished; dinner would begin. As Janine and Nancy stepped away, Jack appeared alongside Maxine and muttered something in her ear that made her eyes turn hard and cold. Nancy considered telling Janine about the fight she'd heard prior to the ceremony and then thought better of it. In just a few more hours, the wedding would be finished. Jack and Maxine would retreat to Manhattan, where they belonged. And Henry and Janine would be allowed to continue their healing journey and budding love.

Nancy was seated with Janine, Henry, Maggie, Rex, and Rex's parents at the family table. Maxine and Jack were located at the far end of the table. Jack's face was rigid, and one could tell he was extremely uncomfortable even though this was his daughter's wedding. As the first glasses of champagne were poured, he clacked his fork and forced the massive crowd to quiet down. Maxine whispered something into his ear, and he gave her a horrible, penetrating look.

Nancy wondered if she'd pleaded with him not to do whatever it was he would do next. Probably, after years of wondering about Jack Potter, years of lusting after him, Maxine now had to face the truth of her actions: that she was involved with a monster masked as a man.

"Good evening, everyone." Jack's voice boomed over the crowd. They directed their attention easily toward him. He was the sort of man you didn't ignore. "I'd like to welcome you all to the wedding of my eldest daughter, Maggie— one of the great loves of my life. Today, we welcome Rex into the family." He lifted his champagne flute toward Rex, who nodded firmly in his direction.

What did Rex think of Jack Potter? He was difficult to read. Probably, he had to show the man unlimited respect for Maggie's sake.

"I just have a few things to say about love," Jack continued.

Nancy's heart pounded, and she downed the rest of her drink to even her nerves. She glanced toward Janine, who looked stricken. Love? How could Jack Potter say anything about love after what he'd done?

"When you find love in your life, you must be brave enough to grab it and never let it go," Jack said. "You have to believe in your heart, in every emotion— and be gentle with yourself as you propel yourself forward through time."

Janine's eyes rimmed with tears as her lips turned up into a sad smirk. Maxine's gaze turned across the table. She seemed to stare directly at Janine. At that moment, Janine caught her eye, as well— and the two women faced off across the family table. All the blood dropped out of Janine's cheeks. Nancy wanted to stand up and punch Jack Potter in the nose. At fifty-nine, did she have the strength for that?

She smiled inwardly at the image of it: the grand-mother of the bride knocking the father of the bride out in front of everyone. What a sight. They would assuredly have a full-page spread in some tabloid. "Grandmother Knocks Out Jack Potter!"

Jack concluded his speech with, "Now, let's enjoy this beautiful evening, shall we?" But in the wake of it, Janine stood and clacked her fork against her glass. Jack turned and scowled at her. His eyes said, "But I've already done the speech. Why do you have to?"

Again, the crowd quieted down for Janine. She lifted her chin regally, like a queen, and began.

"I want to thank you all for coming to my daughter's wedding. It's a day Maggie always dreamed about, so it's been a real struggle to bring this dream to reality. But I think we pulled it off. What do you think, Mags?"

Maggie whistled playfully.

"I think that's a yes," Janine joked. "But in all seriousness, I want to say one thing. When I was a young woman, I gave birth to Maggie and felt immediately like an imposter. How could I possibly bring a baby into the world, let alone figure out how to raise her? How could I possibly fill her head with all the knowledge she needed to get through her life? I worried endlessly about every little detail— from what kind of toothpaste to buy to whether or not I should allow her to ride a bicycle. And you know what? All Maggie ever did back then was look at me and say, 'Mom. I can handle it.' And I feel that in her even now. She's always had a wild independent streak. She's always marched to the beat of her own drum. And when she met Rex and told me she planned to marry him, I asked her, 'Maggie, are you sure? Is this really the one?' And she said, 'Mom. Yes, he is. I can handle it.' And I knew in my heart, she was right; she had this." Janine sucked in a breath, then held her flute even higher toward her daughter. "Maggie, you have made me so proud to call you my daughter. I couldn't ask for anything else other than all the happiness in the world for the two of you. I love you, honey. I love you both so much. To Maggie and Rex!"

Janine's tears streamed down her face as Maggie mouthed, "I love you, Mom," and her own tears cascaded down her cheeks. The crowd clapped wildly for the mother of the bride, who sat and bowed her head, having outdone her ex-husband in speech alone. Jack continued to glower in his corner.

Janine turned her lips toward Nancy's ear and whispered, "At the engagement party, Jack didn't let me give a speech. I wasn't about to let him cut me out this time."

"You showed him," Nancy told her with a wink. "And

his was so boring with no real meaning; it's like he was just there."

Janine's laughter twinkled like music. When she calmed and the first platters were passed around for the first course, she lifted her glass toward Nancy and said, "I can't imagine today without you here, Mom. Thank you. You were always the missing puzzle piece of my life."

Chapter Ten

"You're the grandmother of the bride?" The question was pushed toward her strangely near the drink table. The questioner? One of the Manhattan socialites whom Janine had spent the majority of her twenties and thirties alongside. She ogled Nancy as though she was some sort of prize, then gasped when Nancy nodded. "That's simply insane. Isn't it insane?" the woman asked her friend.

"It's insane," the friend echoed.

Nancy shifted uncomfortably. Her eyes moved just past the woman before her to find another pair of eyes settled upon her with curiosity. They were grayish-green and oddly warm. Their owner was a man who seemed to be in his late fifties, early sixties. His hair was mostly salt on the salt-and-pepper scale, and his skin was tanned and glowing. He had a classic five o'clock stubble, and his lips drew the slightest of crooked smiles, one that seemed especially for her. Nancy felt a strange stab of recognition; she was attracted to this man.

But she hadn't felt that way toward anyone but Neal

in maybe fifteen years. It was unfamiliar territory. And at fifty-nine, she'd expected that sort of thing was a part of her past.

"Tell us. How old are you?" one of the Manhattan socialite friends begged Nancy now.

Nancy had nearly forgotten about them as though they were two flies circling her head.

"The grandmother of the bride, but you look late forties tops," the other affirmed.

"I am decidedly not late forties," Nancy corrected with an ironic laugh. "But I did have my baby at sixteen. I wouldn't recommend it, of course, but it does set you up to be a youthful-looking grandmother."

The women exchanged glances. The one on the left, who wore particularly ridiculous-looking lip-liner, gasped and said, "You had a baby at sixteen?"

This sort of lifestyle was on the trashy side. It didn't happen to "rich" women with other options. Nancy knew this.

"I don't regret it for a second," Nancy told them.

The grayish-green eyes behind them brightened as Nancy stepped around and eased herself alongside the gossiping women, positioning herself directly beside this stranger. She leaned across the bar and ordered herself another vodka tonic as her heart raced.

"Don't you just love people?" The man beside her asked suddenly. His voice was thick and husky.

A laugh erupted from Nancy's throat. She took the vodka tonic and turned to face him. "They can surprise you."

"Those women don't surprise me," the man said as he tilted his head toward the socialites. "I don't think they've had a unique thought in forty years."

"And I suppose you're stirring in unique thoughts?"

"I'm lucky if I have one a month," the man said, chuckling. "But it doesn't mean I don't want to put women like that in their place."

"And where is that— the kitchen?" Nancy asked playfully.

The man laughed outright, smacking his thigh with a heavy hand. Nancy's heart lifted. It had been a long time since she'd flirted. Was that what this was? She thought back to what Alyssa and Maggie had said about her to their friends; she had been this wild child, hadn't she? She had gone all over the world; she'd been with many men. She'd had a way with this sort of thing— and maybe, just maybe, she wasn't too dried up for that sort of thing. Was she?

According to the glow in this man's eyes, she wasn't.

"What are you drinking?" Nancy asked the stranger.

"I haven't quite decided yet," the man told her.

"Yet you look like a guy who always knows what he wants."

"Do I? That's curious. Tell me, then. Tell me what I want."

Nancy's grin widened. They faced off as the band, located on the far end of the dance floor, began to play another song, something Nancy might have wanted to dance to in another era. After all, she had danced her way through the seventies and eighties. She'd always had time to move her hips, get lost in the frenetic beats, and feel as much as she could. She and Neal had never danced much together; theirs had been a passionate relationship of compassion and understanding, with very little "party."

But something about this stranger made her want to dance again.

"I think you want to dance with me," she said suddenly.

His eyes grew wider. "I see you're the kind of woman who likes to take chances."

"I used to be."

"Aren't we always who we used to be?"

"That's a tricky question for another day," Nancy told him. She slipped her hand over his, leading him toward the center of the dance floor. Nancy then eased her hand over his shoulder and shimmied her hips with his. He had a beautiful sense of tempo, and his eyes never left hers as though he was captivated with her.

It was remarkable to feel that she'd captivated someone again. She had thought that sort of thing was lost to another time.

They danced— not just one song, but five in a row. At times, she caught Maggie or Alyssa eyeing her. Both lifted a thumb in support with huge smiles. Janine danced with Henry toward the far end of the dance floor, both lost in one another's eyes. But Nancy wasn't there to fall in love. She was there to have a great time— to feel again. She was there to learn how not to think.

As another song fluttered off, only to be replaced with another, the stranger placed his lips near her ear and said, "I don't suppose I could tempt you with a dance out by the water?"

A previous version of Nancy would have leaped at this idea. Nancy decided to follow that instinct. She nodded and then said, "I don't suppose you'd like to steal us a bottle of wine?"

He winked, then turned toward the open bar. Nancy followed him and watched as he walked around the side of the table, focused on the bartender, who was busy with other customers. In a flash, he gripped one of the bottles of white from the nearest fridge, then rushed out toward the darkness beyond the reception area, where the Nantucket Sound burst out toward the rest of the Atlantic. It was an inky darkness, a nothingness filled with so much. Nancy found strength and a speed within herself that she didn't know she still had. She stretched her legs out vibrantly and chased him to the far dock, where they both collapsed on the sand and giggled like children.

The stranger heaved with last juts of laughter, then inspected the wine bottle.

"Oh no. We need a wine opener," Nancy breathed.

"Not to worry. I was a Boy Scout. Always prepared." He lifted a keychain, on which he had a small wine opener. With a twist of his hand, he drew out the cork, then passed the wine bottle over to Nancy. "Ladies first."

"Some lady. Drinking wine out of the bottle," Nancy quipped with a smile before taking a long swig.

"Desperate times call for desperate measures," he said. "Or whatever they say."

Nancy took one more and then passed the bottle to him. Silence filled the space between them. A small voice in the back of Nancy's mind reminded her that this man was a stranger; she was the bride's grandmother and acting irrationally.

But another voice reminded her of the awaiting test results and that nothing in life was for certain. Time was a finite resource. She would do with it what she could.

"Some wedding, huh?" The stranger said it, then rubbed the back of his hand across his lips.

"Some wedding."

"Lots of gossip swirling around," he said. "About the mother of the bride and the father's girlfriend."

"Yeah, touchy subject," Nancy said.

"Do you think people just get bored and create their own chaos?"

Nancy considered this. "I think I used to do that. I wanted to tell myself a story about myself that interested me. I'm not sure I'm like that now. I don't think that way of living has a lot of longevity. But it's good for a single night, maybe."

"Are you suggesting that's the reason you came out here with me? For the story?" the stranger asked. He then took a swig and grinned that mischievous grin of his.

"Maybe. And maybe I just asked myself if I'd surprised myself recently."

"Do you think it's important to surprise yourself?" he asked.

"Yes, maybe not all the time. But enough."

"Even bad surprises?" he asked.

"Yes, even those." Nancy took the bottle and drank three gulps. The stars above had been to morph and swirl, resulting from her three vodka tonics and several sips of wine. She didn't drink like she used to— thank goodness. But she still felt strange, like a lightweight.

The stranger removed his shoes and stood to place his feet in the rush of the chilly waves. He grimaced, then dropped his head back. "Yow," he said. "That's cold."

"I'm sure it is."

"Join me."

Nancy laughed. "I'm afraid my toes will fall off."

"Trust me," the stranger said. "They won't."

Nancy removed her shoes and stepped alongside him. There, she laced her fingers through his. She was reminded suddenly of the night she'd conceived Janine. There had been similar energy, a similar feeling of leaping into nothingness, as though whatever happened next didn't matter, as long as right now felt just perfect.

"Tell me something real," the man said now, as the waves rushed around their toes and her body quivered in the darkness.

Nancy swallowed sharply. What did she have to lose?

"I'm scared," she breathed. "I know I can't get anything back. And I'm scared I don't have much time left."

Silence filled the space between them again, but it was a comfortable quiet, a thoughtful one.

"It's the worst, isn't it? Getting old?" the stranger asked.

"Maybe, but it has its benefits, too. And I would like to get much, much older." Nancy's eyes filled with tears. "I only just built my relationship with my daughter and granddaughters, and there's so much more to do. My step-daughter, Carmella, and I— well. Things have always been strained, and I ask myself why that is. Maybe there's a way past this. Maybe life is about bettering yourself no matter the chips you're dealt."

"Beautifully said," the man told her.

Nancy stirred with a moment of fear. She had given this man a great deal of herself. She prayed he would tell her something, too. Something that set him apart.

"I'm from the city," he finally mustered. "And I hate so much of my life. I hate that I'm only here for some sort of proof of my social status. I hate money and what money does to your position in society. I hate that I've worked my whole life for this position, only to find out it's not enough."

"Is anything ever enough?" Nancy asked, turning to look at him.

"I don't know. I ask myself that. But if the answer is no, then what do you do? Do you stop living?"

Nancy exhaled through her nose. "I don't know to be honest."

They stepped back from the water, shivering. The man grabbed the bottle of wine and took another swig, then passed it over. Nancy teetered slightly. When she removed the bottle from her lips, she rose on her toes and placed a kiss on this man's lips. She closed her eyes and allowed herself to forget, if only for a moment, that she was a fifty-nine-year-old widow with maybe very little time left.

Right then, she was just Nancy Grimson. It was all she had to be.

"Grandma? Grandma?" The words howled out through the night. Nancy jumped back from the stranger's embrace and turned to face Alyssa and Peter, who'd seemed to have the same idea as Nancy and her stranger. Alyssa had a bottle of wine in one hand and a cheeky smile between her lips. "Grandma, what on earth are you doing out here?"

"Grandma." The stranger echoed the title and gave Nancy a funny smile.

She certainly didn't feel like a grandmother just then.

"And Maddox?" Alyssa turned her attention to the stranger. Her eyes scanned from Maddox to Nancy, then back again as the realization took hold of her. "Wow. Grandma. Did you just go back in time and pull out the wild youthful woman you once were?"

Nancy lifted her chin to catch Maddox's gaze. "My granddaughter knows your name."

Maddox chuckled. He then took another long sip of wine and said, "I've worked with Jack Potter for the past twenty years. I would think his daughters would know my name."

Nancy cackled. It all seemed so ridiculous. "You're friends with the father of the bride?"

"Friend. It's an interesting term, isn't it?"

Nancy's heart swelled at the hilarity of it all. "I suppose we could never work."

"Isn't that the greatest tragedy of all?" Maddox teased.

Alyssa crossed her arms impatiently. She wanted their stance on the beach. Nancy felt unwilling to give it up. But in a moment, Maddox exhaled and said, "I had better head back." Alyssa and Maddox and Peter had broken the perfect spell. It was time to return to reality. How sad.

"I'll join you," Nancy said. "Here's the beach, love. Like grandmother like granddaughter?"

Alyssa tittered as Maddox howled with laughter. "What is happening here on Martha's Vineyard?" he teased as they marched back toward the glow of the reception. "Seems like there's something in the water. The rest of the world's rules just don't apply."

"And thank goodness for that," Nancy said with a crooked grin.

Chapter Eleven

T
he final moments of the reception were filled with snap-shots of beautiful images. Nancy tried to soak up each one, to add them to her ever-growing memory bank. There, Bruce wrapped his arms lovingly around Elsa and whispered something in her ear as the music slowed and shifted them back and forth. Cody and Carmella chatted excitedly at one of the tables, their eyes aglow and cheeks ruddy from alcohol. Maggie remained latched in the arms of her now-husband; her eyelids were half-open as she rolled her head back playfully and spoke to Rex as though they were alone, not in a crowded space. At times, Nancy caught sight of Maddox, that wonderful stranger. Still, he seemed perpetually at a distance, as though they'd gotten too close and now had to ricochet off one another. Nancy remembered this from her previous dating life. Sometimes too much was said or felt at once, and you had to move past that person, like two ships passing in the night.

It was a sad tragedy about love and passion that sometimes it couldn't last.

Toward the end of the night, Nancy found herself again in the ladies' bathroom, peering at a reflection of a funny-looking, wind-swept fifty-nine-year-old lady. Her makeup was smudged. Her hair flowed wildly, like a shampoo commercial, and her lipstick no longer paid any mind to the outline of her lips. She looked passionate and wild— more like a younger version of herself than the woman Neal had married. Maybe that was okay.

"You are not your past," she told the reflection now. "Or are you?"

Maybe you could pick what you wanted to bring with you into the future. Perhaps this wedding had proven something to her about the elements she had missed from the past: the dancing, for one, and the making rash, passionate decisions— kissing strange men on the lips and living to tell the tale.

Nancy began to mop herself up just the slightest bit. After many guests retreated into the night, she knew she and Janine would pile into the same taxi and head home together. She wanted to look the part of a more sophisticated woman if only to avoid questions. She slid a wad of toilet paper beneath her under-eyes as delicately as she could and mopped up the dark ink.

As she worked, several other women came in and out of the bathroom to pee and wash their hands and gossip. Nancy was distracted, so much so that when she realized Maxine was the only other woman in the bathroom, stationed directly beside her at the other sink, her heart nearly shattered with something like fear.

But a moment later, Nancy realized Maxine's face was streaked with black makeup; it was clear she had been crying. Nancy dropped her hands to her sides and watched as Maxine performed a similar cleanup with toilet paper. Only then did Maxine's eyes find Nancy's in the mirror. She nearly jumped from her skin.

"Nancy," Maxine breathed.

"Maxine."

Maxine blinked several times and then dropped her eyes to the ground. After a long pause, she murmured, "That was a beautiful wedding. Wasn't it?"

"Yes, one of the best."

Maxine pressed her lips together. "Maybe it's weird to say, but I always did love Maggie and Alyssa. A lot. I remember so clearly when they were born."

Nancy nodded. "I can't say the same for me. I wasn't around."

Maxine's cheeks brightened to a sterling shade of red. "Funny how things change, I guess."

Nancy couldn't stop herself before she said it. "But you look almost the same as you did when I met you. Or you at least seem the same. I still remember that brash and arrogant little French girl Janine dragged home. I was half out of my mind at any given time, but I had this sense that she was protected when you were around. I knew you had one another's backs."

Nancy hadn't said it as any sort of knife in the back or with any resentment. She'd simply felt the memory and wanted to share it.

"I always loved going to your house," Maxine admitted. "You always had the best snacks."

"Probably the ones most parents wouldn't have allowed in their houses."

"There was a terrific amount of chocolate. That's for sure."

They held one another's gaze for a moment. Maxine lifted her wad of toilet paper and said, "I don't know what kind of novice I am, coming to a wedding without wipes."

"I'm the same."

"At least I'm not alone."

Nancy's heart thudded. In truth, the woman she had witnessed hours earlier being screamed at by Jack Potter had seemed far more alone than ever before.

"You do look remarkable, Nancy," Maxine said then, tenderly. "I know everything was very heavy for you before. In ways that neither Janine nor I could fully comprehend."

Nancy wasn't entirely sure how to answer. Her lips dropped open. Outside, there was the sound of clacking heels, then the boom of a familiar voice. Nancy's brow furrowed as all the color drained from Maxine's cheeks. She leaped for the door and drew it open to find Jack Potter and Janine Grimson Potter— still married and recently separated. Jack had Janine up against a wall, his finger lifted as he hissed at her.

"I don't know where you think you get off saying what you did to my cousin," Jack blared. "And when you stood up to make that speech? Do you know how much you embarrassed me?"

Janine's nostrils flared with rage. "Step back, Jack. Get out of my face."

"I paid for every single minute of this godforsaken wedding," Jack growled as he shifted his weight to his other foot.

Maxine and Nancy stood off to the side of the bathroom door. Nancy's heart raced as Maxine seemed to allow herself to be swallowed up. Her shoulders fell forward, and she looked like a wilting flower.

"I hardly protested when Maggie wanted to move this shindig to this stupid island," Jack continued. "I went along with it, but now I get here, and you want to mock me and say stuff about me to my family members and—"

"That's enough, Jack! Anything I said about you was true. And you know that," Janine blared, trying to hold her stance.

"Shut up, Janine. Can't you ever shut your mouth?"

Toward the far end of the hallway, Maggie and Alyssa appeared. They walked hand in hand, both giggling like little girls and staggering slightly on their heels. Nancy bolted toward Jack and Janine with a single mission: she had to break up this fight if only so Maggie wouldn't remember this moment and associate it with her wedding day.

Plus, she felt endlessly protective of her daughter.

"Jack Potter." Nancy stomped up directly beside him and shoved his shoulder the slightest bit back so that his eyes found hers.

"Get away from me, old lady."

Nancy set her jaw. "You will not make a scene at your daughter's wedding. Not like this. You've already done enough to ruin this family because you lack self-control, empathy, and many other things decent people offer the world. Get away from my daughter. Take your girlfriend, and go."

Jack's face grew shadowed. His eyes peered beyond Nancy, finding Alyssa and Maggie, still far enough away that they didn't understand what was happening.

At that moment, Nancy realized that Maddox was in earshot. He lurked near the men's bathroom, his hands in his pockets. He gave her that smile again, then winked.

Jack lifted his chin as though poised to give Nancy the

ultimate insult, the kind of thing that would destroy her. But instead, he turned and gripped Maxine's hand angrily. "Let's get out of here," he told her. He then stormed down the hallway toward Maggie, paused, hugged her, and said what appeared to be kind words. Nancy couldn't hear them.

Meanwhile, Janine quivered against the wall. She buzzed her lips and then said, "I don't know what came over me. I felt like my old self. The one who was always slightly afraid of Jack Potter. The one who wanted our marriage to work so badly, I let him do and say whatever he pleased."

This broke Nancy's heart in two. "You should have called me years ago. You should have asked for help."

But of course, why would Janine have done that? There had been too much bad blood between them, and it was all Nancy's fault. Maybe the fact that Jack existed at all in Janine's life was all Nancy's fault. Her heart felt so battered, so ominous. Her eyes returned to Maddox's. He nodded with approval, then turned and walked down the hallway, soon disappearing into the darkness of the night. Nancy had a feeling she would never see him again.

She was grateful that this could be his last memory of her, though. An image of a strong and powerful woman, one who'd put Jack Potter in his place. She wanted to be remembered for everything she had done that night. She'd felt complete, with the best elements of her previous life and her current one all rolled up together as one. She felt free.

"Are you okay?" Nancy finally asked as she wrapped her arms around Janine.

"I am. I won't let him get to me."

Maggie and Alyssa appeared alongside them.

"Is this a family group hug?" Alyssa asked.

Nancy turned her head and then nodded. "Get in here, girls."

Maggie and Alyssa joined in. They were the beautiful Grimson-Remington-Potter girls all latched together, in a flurry of emotion, perfume, and makeup, something uniquely theirs. Nancy's heart swelled at the immensity of love she had for all of them.

When their hug broke, Alyssa yawned and stretched her arms over her head. "I think it's time for me to sleep."

"I have to find Rex," Maggie stated as she looked around.

"You've already lost your husband? It's only been a few hours," Alyssa returned.

"Last I saw him, he was doing a very embarrassing dance with the other groomsmen," Maggie said. "I just couldn't take it."

"Uh-oh. Are you going to leave him?" Alyssa asked.

Maggie rolled her eyes and stepped back toward the reception area. More and more guests had begun to filter out, either headed to their hotel rooms or back to their other residences on Martha's Vineyard. Maggie lifted her dress and fled for the reception area to find Rex. Alyssa dallied behind and reported that she'd already broken things off with Peter.

"He just wasn't who I thought he was," she said as she walked alongside her mother.

Janine laughed heartily. "You're still only twenty-two. I suppose you have a lot more men to meet along the way."

"Oh great." Alyssa sighed. "More men to disappoint me."

"Not all of them are so disappointing," Janine insisted. "I met Henry, didn't I?"

"Henry is an artistic saint," Alyssa affirmed. "Oh, did you see Dad's face when he saw you with Henry? I mean, they used to work together, right?"

Janine was silent for a moment. "Your father used to help sponsor some of Henry's documentaries. He thought Henry was a genius, and he is, but I'm not with Henry to get back at your father."

Alyssa thought for a moment, then added, "But it doesn't hurt."

Janine laughed good-naturedly. "I can't fight that. It doesn't hurt. That's for sure."

Back at the house, Nancy, Janine, Carmella, Elsa, Mallory, and Alyssa all changed out of their dresses and gathered for tea and hot cocoa on the back porch. They wrapped themselves in flannel blankets and swapped stories from the previous hours.

"I miss Maggie," Alyssa admitted as she placed her empty mug on the table.

"Oh, you girls will see each other just the same," Janine offered. "You're neighbors in the city."

"I know. But the next part could be rough. Once there's marriage, then what? Babies? Big moves to stupid places like San Francisco or Seattle?"

"They'd better not move anywhere," Janine warned in a way that seemed only half a joke.

"I don't know. I can't let her go." Alyssa stuck her lower lip out and exhaled.

"It'll be okay. What you and Maggie have is special," Carmella affirmed. She then lifted her eyes toward Elsa and winked, proof that their relationship continued to grow intimate and more powerful. "Rex is nothing compared to what you girls have."

"I hope you're right," Alyssa replied. "If she pulls back, I'll just break into her house and demand squatter's rights. She can't get away from me, even if she tries."

Chapter Twelve

Alyssa bounded down the steps the following morning and flung herself into Maggie's arms. Maggie nearly fell back as Alyssa howled, "She did it! She lost her virginity!" Maggie's eyes rolled into the back of her head as Rex scrambled to keep Maggie upright. Nancy watched from the porch and joined in Maggie's laughter as Janine, Carmella, and Elsa padded out onto the porch as well.

"What's gotten into you?" Janine called.

"Don't you dare tell her what you said," Maggie hissed at Alyssa.

"I just wished her a happy marriage, Mom," Alyssa called as she stepped back from Maggie, then adjusted a curl around her sister's ear. "You ready for breakfast? We've slaved away for you two since the crack of dawn."

"She talks like she's helped at all," Janine said. She stepped down and hugged her eldest, then greeted Rex warmly. "We have fresh croissants from the Sunrise Cove and plenty of donuts, eggs, bacon, and sausage and such. Carmella and Elsa have done the brunt of the work, and

Grandma Nancy, of course." She turned and winked toward Nancy as Nancy's heart swelled.

How she loved caring for her girls like this. She lifted her chin skyward and admired the fluff of a September cloud as it crept back out toward the ocean. Yet again, she thought of Neal, of how pleased he would have been to know all this love bubbled within his house. Before she'd moved in, he'd described how desolate the place had been years before, when Elsa and Carmella had been young and their brother had died in a horseback riding accident. Shortly after, a car accident had claimed their mother. "It was as though a dark cloud existed over the top of us for years," Neal had described. "But with you here, the dark cloud has passed away."

"Don't call her Grandma Nancy. That woman is no grandmother," Alyssa said as they entered the back porch area, where Carmella and Elsa had already set the table.

"Why not?" Janine asked.

Alyssa waggled her eyebrows. Nancy shook her head wildly so that her hair wafted around her ears.

"What?" Alyssa asked mischievously. "You don't want me to tell them I caught you making out with a handsome guy by the water?"

Janine's jaw dropped. Elsa clapped her hand over her mouth while Carmella burst into laughter. Baby Zachery let out a wild screech in Mallory's arms as all eyes continued to dig into Nancy.

"Alyssa. Why did you tell on me?" Nancy cried as she looked at each woman who now stared at her for an explanation.

"The world deserves to know what a badass you are," Alyssa affirmed, her smirk plastered on her face. "Peter and I thought we were so cool, stealing a bottle of wine from the bar and going to make out by the water. Little did we know, Nancy here already had that idea up her sleeve."

Nancy's cheeks burned. She knew they were bright red.

Janine clucked her tongue as a smile spread wider. "You can take the girl out of the madness, but you can't take the madness out of the girl."

"What? It was a wedding! I was all hyped up on love and excitement and all that jazz," Nancy shot playfully.

"Yeah, yeah," Elsa teased. "We get it. You're so wild and free, even at fifty-nine, and we're just as lame as ever."

"I didn't say any of you were lame." Nancy leaned back in her chair and ran a hand through her hair. "You girls, I swear."

"It was implied by how much cooler you are than us," Janine pointed out.

"Good grief." But Nancy couldn't get the smile off her face throughout breakfast. It pleased her to know that they thought of her this way, even if they teased her.

They ate a sinful breakfast— oozing droplets of honey across their croissants and eating greasy sausages and laughing until their stomachs ached. Outside, a late September wind forced the waves to crash against the beach and the trees to extend toward the ground below. Elsa suggested they all go for a walk to stretch their legs, and everyone hustled into their autumn jackets and padded off the porch and toward the waterline.

"You coming, Teenage Nancy?" Alyssa teased.

Even as Nancy smiled down at her beautiful grand-daughter, another crashing wave of fatigue came over her. She shook her head delicately. "I don't think so, honey."

"Too much wine last night?"

"Something like that," Nancy said. "I have to rest up for my next adventure."

"Suit yourself." Alyssa then hustled up to walk alongside Mallory, where she lifted baby Zachery from her arms and draped him across her shoulder.

Again, Nancy's heart swelled, even as she swam through this horrific wave of pain and fear.

With everyone gone, she stepped back into the shadows of the house. Dishes pushed above the sink-line, but she knew they could wait. Nancy leaned against the doorway and tried to will this current wave away from her. Maybe all this could be solved with mind over matter. She had once watched a special about hypnosis on PBS, which had explained that so much of the mind was at a distance from you, but if you could tap into whatever that other stuff was, you could have much more control over your health and well-being.

Maybe she could break into that darkness and convince her health to return to normal.

But as the minutes passed, fear wrapped itself around Nancy's throat and threatened to make her tumble to the ground. Her shoulders sagged forward, and tears fell. A sob escaped her throat, one that ricocheted and echoed through the entire house. She clenched her eyes closed tightly and thanked her lucky stars that the rest of her family was out in the wild salty winds rather than there to watch her break down.

"Nancy? Is that you?"

It was some kind of trick, wasn't it? Nancy's eyes popped open as she turned to find Carmella. She stepped out from the living area, rubbing her own eyes.

"Oh. I thought you'd gone with the others." Nancy's voice sounded like she had been taken off guard. In truth,

Carmella was the very last person of the group she wanted to interact with at that moment. She felt she couldn't be fully honest with her, as they'd never had much to say to one another. Plus, Carmella went through so many dark moods, ones Nancy wasn't entirely sure she could carry at the moment.

But Carmella stepped toward her as her eyebrows lowered. "Nancy, are you okay?"

Nancy's chin quivered. She rubbed at one of her eyes and willed herself to stop crying. Why didn't she have more control? Why did she always fall apart?

Carmella came closer. When she stood a foot away from her, Nancy removed her hand again and let Carmella find the full view of her tear-blotched face. She knew she looked like a mess. She felt suddenly vulnerable.

"Nancy. Is it the wedding?" Carmella breathed. "Janine? Jack? What is it?"

Nancy flared her nostrils. She felt utterly cornered. She wouldn't have shown all this emotion outwardly if she had known someone else was home.

"I just don't want to miss anything else," Nancy finally blurted.

Carmella nodded. "I can understand that."

Nancy knew, in a sense, Carmella could. She had spent so much of her life at a distance from her family, only to recently find her way back to them. Nancy turned back and headed toward the sink, just wanting to do something with her hands. She yanked open the faucet and stared straight ahead as she scrubbed one plate after another. Carmella stood alongside her to take the clean plates and dry them off. They worked like that for a full five minutes before Nancy burst into tears again.

Carmella turned off the faucet and placed a hand on Nancy's upper back.

"You can talk to me about it. Whatever it is."

Nancy swallowed the lump in her throat and stepped back toward the kitchen table. There, she collapsed and placed her face in her hands.

"I'm just so scared, Carmella."

Carmella sat opposite her at the small table. Both of her hands were across the wood, her fingers spread apart. She looked anxious but present.

"You can tell me why you're scared if you want to."

Nancy pressed her lips together. After a pause, she breathed, "Are you sure?"

"For years, nobody asked me what was wrong. If someone had, maybe I could have resolved some of my issues earlier," Carmella admitted.

"About Colton?"

"About all of it," Carmella told her. "Therapy has helped. And Cody and Elsa have lifted me up the past few months. But it's led me to have more compassion for myself and others. No matter what you're dealing with, you shouldn't keep it bottled up so tightly inside. It could destroy you."

"I just— I feel that I lost so much over the years," Nancy whispered. "I gave up on so much. I failed Janine over and over again. Your father gave me a new life, and then he passed away. I tried to use his strength to bring my worlds back together again."

"And you succeeded," Carmella pointed out. "Janine, Maggie, and Alyssa are all here. They're here because of you and Dad."

Nancy nodded. She swallowed the lump in her throat

as another tear rolled down her cheek. "Something's wrong with me, Carmella. Really wrong."

Carmella furrowed her brow. "What do you mean?"

"I just mean that my body isn't quite right. I've noticed it for months but tried to ignore it. I told myself I just needed to drink more water or stretch more or get more sleep. But the truth of it is, I don't know what's wrong with me, and the doctor spouted out a whole list of possible things— including the big C-word."

Carmella's eyes closed gently. Her shoulders sagged forward. "God, Nancy. I had no idea."

Nancy was surprised that in the wake of acknowledging this truth, she felt a tiny bit lighter. She felt freer.

The truth. It was really powerful.

"I had a lot of tests done," Nancy told her. "I'm just hanging in there until I know for sure what's going on. I should be getting the results soon. And until then, all I can do is imagine the worst."

"I can understand that," Carmella told her. "I'm sure your mind is playing a million little tricks on you. And I also understand why you don't want the girls to know yet."

Nancy nodded as tears welled yet again in her eyes. "I just don't know what to do about it."

"You can wait as long as you want. It's your choice," Carmella said. "But just know that I will keep your secret safe. I promise."

Nancy sniffled. After a long pause, she whispered, "I can't even begin to thank you, Carmella. Really."

"It's my honor," Carmella told her. "I know what it's like to need to keep things separate from those you care about the most. It's a tricky balancing act." Her smile faltered the slightest bit as she added, "And what about that man from last night? Does this have anything to do with that?"

Nancy buzzed her lips as a wave of foolishness crashed over her. "Oh, I don't know. I guess I just thought if I lived youthfully, I could outrun this fear of death somehow."

"I understand that. Maybe it works sometimes. Who's to say?"

A few moments later, the others appeared on the back porch. Nancy rushed back to the sink to continue the dishes as Alyssa and Maggie rushed in. Alyssa screeched that she'd cut open her finger on a rock, while Maggie explained there wasn't even a droplet of blood. The others appeared, greeting Nancy and Carmella brightly. It was decided that wine would soon be poured and mimosas would be made. The celebration wasn't yet over. And Nancy told herself she was allowed to hide in this joy for a little while longer. She would face the horrors of everything else later when she had to. Maybe tomorrow. Or perhaps the week after that.

Chapter Thirteen

J anine and Nancy hovered in the produce aisle at the Edgartown grocery store as Elsa padded her fingers over various mangoes, apples, and nectarines. Nancy gripped the grocery cart so tightly that all the blood drained from her fingers. Elsa and Bruce had just gotten into a little spat outside of the Lodge— one in full view of Nancy and Janine, and nobody knew quite what to say about it. Elsa looked shaken. She lifted a nectarine, tossed it lightly in her hand, and said, "I didn't think Bruce and I would ever fight."

"That's what couples do," Janine pointed out. She grabbed a bag of apples and tilted her head to catch Elsa's gaze. "Seriously. And you and Bruce have been dating for long enough now that maybe it was time to see how the two of you handled a dispute."

Elsa arched her eyebrow but dropped her gaze. "It was stupid, too. He had to change our plans. It happens all the time. I just haven't been sleeping well the past few nights, and I had this sudden fear that he would abandon me. Isn't that ridiculous? I guess it's because I've hardly dated in my life. Aiden was it for me. I don't know what it means when, you know, a text message goes unanswered, or he suddenly has to change plans."

Nancy caught Janine's gaze and shrugged. Fear permeated Elsa's face. Nancy could understand the emotion behind this. Before Neal, she'd felt tossed around by men who said one thing one day and did a far different thing the next. Still, she didn't believe Bruce was this sort of man. He had far too much compassion. And besides, like Elsa, he was an islander. Islanders weren't cruel to other islanders.

Elsa's face scrunched up tightly. She yanked herself around and marched directly toward the wine section. Nancy and Janine walked slowly, side by side, allowing Elsa to take the lead.

"I've never seen her so dramatic before," Janine breathed. "It's almost refreshing to see. She's always been a type A creature to me."

Nancy laughed under her breath. "Neal said she was always that way. Very goal-oriented and never obsessed with boys."

Elsa collected three bottles of wine, then placed them tenderly into the bottom of the grocery cart even as Nancy reminded her they had plenty of wine back at the house. Elsa's expression was sharp.

"We're going to need it," she said sharply.

When they reached the line for the cashier, Nancy shifted her weight as Janine lifted her phone to text Maggie back, who was on day three of her beautiful honeymoon with Rex. Their plan was a trip to the French Riviera for two weeks, followed by a brief stint back in New York City, then a whole month in Southeast Asia, where they planned to travel in a more "rugged" fashion. Maggie had suggested she wanted to sleep on the beach, only for Janine to nearly have a heart attack and beg her to stay in hostels, at least. Maggie had laughed and said, "I just wanted to see your face when I said that."

"She's having the trip of a lifetime," Janine said now as she tilted her phone screen over for Nancy to see. Maggie and Rex stood on the beach, arm in arm; Maggie wore a bright yellow bikini, highlighting her beautiful abs and long legs, while Rex had on a pair of black swim trunks.

"Look at them," Nancy breathed. "Their kids are going to be supermodels."

Janine blushed as she slipped her phone back into her purse. "Your great-grandchildren, you mean?"

Nancy cackled at the thought. "Don't make me feel older than I already do."

Janine's eyes flickered up toward the magazine rack. Nancy watched as her expression faded from one of joy to one of complete and unadulterated horror. Her arms fell to her sides. "No." She ripped a magazine from the rack and lifted it toward them both.

There on the front cover was a near-perfect photograph of the events that had transpired at Maggie's wedding the previous Saturday. Off to the left, Jack Potter and Maxine Aubert stood, regal and proud and arrogant-looking, with Maxine's arm snaked through Jack's. A few feet away, Maggie and Janine stood, both with red blotchy cheeks and eyes.

"No," Janine whispered again. She covered her mouth with her hand in mock horror as Nancy watched her stare at the cover.

Alongside the photograph were large words—"Manhattan Socialite Wedding of the Decade," alongside presumably made-up quotes from the tabloid magazine itself.

"GET AWAY FROM ME AND MY DAUGHTER!" cried a terrifying Janine Potter at her daughter Maggie's wedding.

The Manhattan Socialite Wedding of the Decade was slated by some as being upward of three million.

"I NEVER LOVED YOU," Jack Potter blared back as he protected his new love, Janine's ex-best friend, Maxine.

Janine's hand shook as she took in this full view of the fictionalized version of her life. "Those bastards. They just make up whatever they want to sell magazines."

Elsa and Nancy peered over Janine's shoulders to take in more of the photos within the magazine itself— photos that caught Jack looking rogue, arrogant, and mean and photos that made Janine look weak and sometimes "fatter" than she actually was.

"Janine is out of control," says a source close to the family.

Slowly, Janine placed the magazine on the conveyer belt and watched as the cashier scanned it. The cashier did a double take on the magazine cover and the woman before him but knew better than to say anything. Elsa paid for the wine and the magazine, gathered everything in her arms, and headed out to the car. Nancy and Janine walked behind her, both zombie-like.

"I don't know what to do," Janine whispered as they hovered outside Elsa's car in the parking lot. "I never know what to tell Alyssa and Maggie, especially when they air our dirty laundry out like that."

"They're much stronger than we know," Nancy told her. "I'm sure they know how crazy it all is."

"Yes, but so much of it is true," Janine whispered. "There was a big fight. Jack did belittle me in front of a number of people. Yes, they doctored those photos, but they also captured the actual story, in a way."

"But what do you care, Janine?" Nancy asked. "So what if people need gossip. But you don't need those people. You have us. You have the Lodge."

Elsa sniffled as she shot into the driver's seat. "The only antidote I know for our day's problems is many, many glasses of wine." She then revved the engine as Nancy and Janine hustled to jump in and get their seat belts fastened.

"I'll alert the others. We need girl time," Nancy said as she lifted her phone to text Mallory and Carmella. "Dinner and drinks at the house tonight. We have a lot to talk about."

Nancy hadn't had real girlfriends throughout her teenage years and into her twenties and thirties. It had always seemed outside of the bounds of her own life, the ways of women together— especially women who cared for one another. Now, as she sat at the porch table surrounded by some of the women she loved most, she felt this shell of comfort around them as they swapped stories and made one another laugh; nothing in the outside world could touch them.

"I just don't know what to do about him," Elsa blared since it was her turn to complain. She lifted the wine bottle and poured a big helping for herself, then tilted the wine so that it circled around and around the glass. "I do care about him, but right now, it's just so complicated."

She then turned her eye toward Mallory, her daughter, and asked, "And what's up lately with Lucas, Mal? I haven't seen him around much."

Mallory's nostrils flared. "He's such an idiot. Always telling me he wants to work harder to make us a better family, then always letting me down!"

"Men!" Janine clucked as she lifted her wineglass higher. She took a sip, then glanced toward the porch door. "Where is Carmella, anyway? We need as many of the Grimson-Remington gang as we can get."

"You're right. There's strength in numbers," Nancy affirmed.

"I think the worst part about all of this is knowing that I spent so many years of my life loving that man," Janine said somberly. "I want to go back to my twenty-five-year-old self and ask her if she's really happy. Do I remember any of it correctly? Or was I just sleepwalking through my life, complacent?"

"You clearly weren't sleepwalking," Elsa pointed out. "You raised two beautiful daughters. They're striking and intelligent and bring so much to the world around them. A sleepwalking mother wouldn't have allowed that."

Nancy's heart thudded in her chest. Had she been sleepwalking through her early motherhood? A bit. Yes, a bit. Fear and regret swirled through her stomach and chest. She sipped the rest of her wineglass back and stood on shaky legs. She would just go inside for a moment to regroup.

"Are you going to start dinner?" Elsa asked.

"I'll get to it in a second," Nancy returned as she staggered toward the back porch.

"Why don't we just order something?" Elsa suggested. She stood and walked into the house after Nancy. She seemed not to notice Nancy's weakness. Perhaps Nancy was just good at hiding it.

"I'll grab the menus in the kitchen," Elsa announced.

"Great, honey." Nancy continued toward the staircase, where she gripped the railing and nearly fell to the ground. Out the window, she spotted Cody's car. In the frame of the window, Cody pressed his lips over Carmella's before Carmella leaped out of the vehicle and headed for the door. It warmed Nancy to know Carmella would soon be amongst them. She was the only one with her secret. There was safety in that.

Nancy eased her way up the staircase to take a Tylenol and drink a bottle of water. As she sat at the edge of her bed, she felt her consciousness take hold of her again. Her thoughts seemed firm and alive. Again, she could rejoin her daughters downstairs; she could find space and strength to belittle Jack Potter and his selfish decisions. She could find a way to demonize Bruce Holland, even though she didn't feel it, even a bit, in the depths of her soul.

Sometimes women just needed to rant. They needed to support one another as the harshness of the world pressed down upon them. They needed to swap tips about face creams and pedicures and shapewear, and they needed to do it in the space of safety and love.

Nancy stepped back toward the staircase, lifted her chin regally, and then padded down toward the porch. Elsa was no longer in the kitchen; probably, she'd headed out to the porch to ask everyone what they wanted to order. Nancy drew open the door between the house and the porch, then stopped dead in her tracks.

The sight she'd left was not the one she now found.

Janine pressed her hands over her eyes as horrible, tender wails escaped her throat. Carmella stood alongside her with her hand over her shoulder while Elsa shed her tears off to the right. Mallory looked stricken; all the blood had drained from her cheeks as baby Zachery slept on her shoulder, his lips parted.

"Janine? Elsa?" Nancy's voice cracked.

Carmella lifted her eyes toward Janine's. They were filled with sadness, rimmed red. Silence ballooned around them.

Finally, Janine dropped her hands from her eyes and turned her blotchy face toward her mother's.

"When were you going to tell us about these tests?" she demanded.

Nancy's jaw dropped. Carmella stepped back from Janine, her hands in the air. Nancy felt the colossal weight of betrayal.

"Why did you tell her, Carmella?" Her voice cracked.

Carmella stuttered. "I thought that's why everyone was so upset. I thought that's why we met today. I misunderstood."

Nancy's throat tightened. She could just imagine it now: Carmella coming home to find Janine all out of sorts on the back porch.

"She just looked at me and said, 'We don't know anything for sure yet,'" Janine whispered now, as still more tears rolled down her cheeks. "And I knew. I knew you'd lied to me. I thought we said we would be honest with one another now, Mom! After all we've been through. I thought we had gotten to a point in our relationship where we could face things head-on together."

Nancy dropped her chin. She couldn't imagine a single thing to say that would fix this. Then filled with vitriol, she lifted her eyes back toward Carmella and muttered, "I can't believe you, Carmella. But I guess I should have known."

Carmella's eyes darkened. She slipped away from the porch table, whipped her hands into the air, then hustled away from the porch, wrapping around the house toward the front driveway. Nancy's heart shattered. Only a few days after she and Carmella had repaired their relationship, it had exploded all over again.

And now, she had a devastated and fearful Janine and Elsa on her hands, on top of her mental instability.

It would be a long night.

Chapter Fourteen

Janine lurked outside the yoga studio the following morning. Nancy eyed her as she finalized her session. She pressed her palms together and wished the eight women who'd appeared for the early-morning yoga class a beautiful day ahead. "Remember. You are not your past," she told them. This time, she felt akin to a hypocrite as she said it; after all, if anything, the past haunted her more than ever these days. Perhaps you could never escape it.

When the Katama guests disappeared down the hallway, Janine slipped through the doorway and lifted her chin to greet her mother. She held a box of donuts and placed them tenderly at the center of Nancy's desk. Even still, she struggled to meet her eye. It had been two days since Carmella had broken the news of Nancy's potential health problems, and Janine had required several conversations, many of them tear-filled or scream-filled. "Why didn't you tell me? All we've done is repair our relationship over the past few months. All we've done is grow closer. And now, it's like all that work has flown out the window."

Now, Janine spoke into the donut box. "I'm sorry about some of the stuff I said last night."

Nancy blew out the air from between her lips. She lifted a donut to her mouth, took a small bite, then placed the chocolate-glazed monster back in its place. "Like I told you before, there's nothing we can do about it right now. The test results aren't back."

"The waiting is just so awful." Janine crossed and uncrossed her arms. Outside, the wind howled against the glass and whipped through the trees. "Did you see the news? They think a tropical storm might come through." Her eyes twitched.

"I saw." Nancy leaned against the desk and considered the waves from Katama Bay as they crashed against the far dock.

"Are you used to big storms like this?"

"We've had a few," Nancy replied. "Neal and Elsa arranged for a safe house for everyone at the Katama Lodge. If it gets too bad..."

"We'll bring everyone up there?"

"Yeah, and ourselves," Nancy affirmed. "And there's enough food up there to last us, just in case things get particularly dire."

"What do you mean? What could happen?"

"If the electricity goes out, if we don't have water for a few days..." Nancy shrugged, even as her heart sped up with a sudden jolt of worry.

"Have you ever had to take the guests there?"

"No. Never." Nancy's nostrils flared. She lifted the same chocolate-glazed donut and took three large bites in a row. Sugar rolled across her tongue, and her thoughts stirred wildly. "But it's business as usual until we make the call, okay?"

Janine squinted out at the angry ocean. "I'll keep an eye on the weather."

"Thank you." Nancy chewed somberly, then asked, "Are you feeling okay? After that tabloid magazine?"

"That's the thing about tabloid magazines, isn't it? They're big news for one day and one day only. I should have remembered that when we found the magazine. Already, the grocery store doesn't have that issue in stock. Probably by next week, everyone will have forgotten my name again. And it helps not to be in the city. I have this whole life here. I have you. And I have Elsa and Carmella."

Nancy's heart thudded. "Carmella. I haven't seen her since—"

"I know. Me neither," Janine said. "Elsa said she'd rearranged a lot of her schedule to avoid seeing us. I think she feels guilty for revealing your secret like that."

Nancy's first instinct was to say she should feel guilty. *She promised me! She promised to keep my secret safe!*

But revenge and vitriol were elements of her old life. They had no use here— not in her world of compassion and empathy and forgiveness.

"It's always been such a mess between Carmella and me," Nancy said softly.

Janine nodded. "The longer I stay with all of you here, the more I get that sense. But Elsa and Carmella have both given me their versions of their life stories. They're complicated, to say the least. You fell into an already poisonous environment. You can't blame yourself for not being equipped to fix every element of it."

Heels clacked down the hallway to reveal Elsa, her

cheeks porcelain and pale and her eyes enormous, like saucers. "Have you seen the news about this storm?"

"We were just talking about it," Janine told her.

Elsa slipped her fingers through her hair. "It's just been that kind of year, hasn't it? One thing after another." She stepped toward the window and watched the waterline. "Bruce hasn't stopped calling since yesterday."

"And have you answered?" Nancy asked.

Elsa shrugged like a teenager. "I have. I just don't know. I ask myself if I want to get my heart broken all over again, you know?"

"But Elsa, Aiden didn't break your heart. Not on purpose," Nancy said softly. She placed her hand over Elsa's shoulder and added, "He loved you with everything he had. And maybe Bruce could do that, too."

Elsa crossed her arms tightly over her chest. She looked closed-off, like a frightened animal cornered by a pack of wolves. "Maybe it's all too soon. I don't know."

Again, a strong gust of wind rushed against the windows and whipped across the trees. Nancy shivered.

"It's not going to be pretty," Elsa said as she nodded toward the brewing weather. "I have a feeling we'll have a whole lot of chaos on our hands. So I think I'll tell the staff to start battening down the hatches."

Elsa turned and walked back toward the hallway. Just before she disappeared, Nancy asked, "Have you seen Carmella at all today?"

Elsa shook her head. She turned and made heavy eye contact with Nancy, then added, "She probably just needs time. The way she feels guilt is enormous. She's frozen with it. But if you coax her out, bit by bit—"

Nancy nodded. "It's always like starting from scratch with her."

"No. Not anymore," Elsa said. "She's timid and frightened, but she's also attacking the problem head-on with therapy." She again glanced toward the window, where a bird whipped past, struggling against the winds. "Once we get through this tropical storm, we'll have another girls' night— just the Remington-Grimson girls. And whatever happens with those tests, we'll attack that head-on, too. We're stronger together."

Elsa then disappeared into the shadows of the hallway. Nancy collapsed into the chair alongside her desk and dropped her chin to her chest.

"I have to get going," Janine told her. "I have a client at eight and another at nine." She paused, dropped her teeth over her lower lip, then added, "Are you going to be okay? Do you need anything?"

Nancy wanted to point out that these sorts of questions were the very things she'd wanted to avoid; she hadn't wanted pity. On the contrary, she had wanted to wade through these potential horrors until the very last minute to pretend everything was all right.

"I'll be fine," she told Janine, her words pointed. "Good luck today."

Janine nodded. "You too."

Chapter Fifteen

By four in the afternoon, the Weather Channel illustrated a far different picture of the approaching storm. The consensus was that it was on its way full force, and it had the potential to be dangerous. Elsa sent a text alert to all of the women at the Katama Lodge, which demanded their presence in the large dining hall, where they would receive instructions about the hours ahead. Nancy hovered toward the back of the dining area and watched as, one after the other, women in their late twenties to late fifties entered the dining hall, many in athletic wear with their eyes enormous as they whispered about the potential threat of the storm.

"Do you think the Lodge is high enough? Is there a potential for flooding?" This came from a woman in her mid-forties, a woman incredibly prone to anxiety, who had stayed at the Lodge far beyond what Janine had recommended, as she feared returning home and slipping back into her anxious waves of depression. She simply couldn't get it into her head that she had to return home.

The Lodge had become her refuge, and she had enough money to keep that going. Nancy had heard she was an heiress.

"It's difficult to say how the storm will affect us," Nancy told her. "It depends on several factors. But, luckily, we have a place to take all of you. We'll outline the procedure shortly, but for now, if you could please sit down?"

The heiress certainly didn't look made of money, not then. She teetered slightly onto her toes as her lower lip bubbled around. Nancy wanted to tell this girl to pull herself together, but she wanted to scream the words to herself, as well. Everything seemed just as tumultuous as the weather outside, with no clear end in sight.

Elsa appeared in the doorway. All the blood had drained from her cheeks, and she seemed unwilling to return. Just after her, Bruce Holland appeared. His shoulders were broad and powerful, his face stern. Elsa whipped around and lifted her chin toward him as her eyes swam with tears. Nancy could just barely make out what she said then.

"I have to take care of these people."

"But who will take care of you?" Bruce asked. His hand splayed over her cheek. "You're so goddamn proud all the time. You don't have to be, you know."

Elsa's chin quivered. Bruce hadn't allowed the rift between them to continue. Instead, he'd taken everything into his own hands and forced Elsa to see the truth: that he was falling in love with her. He didn't want to hurt her. It was pure, and it was messy, and maybe that was all that the world could offer any of them just then.

As if on cue, rain splattered across the tall windows that wrapped out from the grand dining hall and offered a sterling view of the Katama Bay, which now seemed so volatile and violent in the fresh hours of the storm.

Bruce lowered his lips over Elsa's, and they kissed tenderly, their eyes closed, as more and more guests from the Katama Lodge entered the dining room to await instructions. Nancy turned her eyes from Elsa and Bruce and found Janine beside her, her brow furrowed as she typed furiously on her phone.

"I just want to make sure Henry knows he can come to our safe house," she explained. "I'm worried about him."

"Of course. Do you have the address?"

Janine nodded. "Mallory gave it to me. He said he wanted to get some footage of the storm for his documentary, which is crazy. I told him that being an artist doesn't mean risking your life. And he then gave me a whole list of artists who have risked their lives in the name of art. I told him the difference is that I, Janine Grimson, wasn't dating any of those people. He hasn't texted back since."

"Ugh. I'm so sorry." Nancy's heart rattled with worry. "I've sent Carmella several messages as well, but none of them have gone through. I'm worried we won't have cell service soon."

Janine pressed her lips into a fine line. "She hasn't responded to my messages, either."

"This is ridiculous." Nancy yanked her phone from her pocket and dialed Carmella's number. It didn't even ring; it went straight to voicemail. Of course, in this day and age, Nancy knew better than to leave a voicemail. "Shoot."

Elsa hustled to the front of the dining hall. She spread her hands out in front of her like a preacher and asked the women to quiet down. Slowly, the gossip and murmurs halted. They turned their eyes toward Elsa like frightened kindergarteners.

"Good afternoon, everyone. As you can see, we have something of a storm on our hands." Elsa clasped her fingers together too tightly; her anxiety swelled off her in waves. "We have several buses on their way to the Katama Lodge. They will drive all of us over to the safe house, which is located far from the waterline. My father had it built for this very reason."

Several of the women exchanged worried looks. Some gasped outrageously as though they thought they were being recorded. Finally, one woman raised a frail hand to ask if they could collect their valuables from their suites and cabins prior to departure. Elsa said yes as long as they hurried back.

"The storm is about to get much stronger, and we need to get over to the safe house as soon as we can," Elsa informed them.

As the women hustled back to their rooms, three Lodge staff members gathered to mount storm-protecting walls over the large window of the dining area. As the walls were mounted, Nancy's sinister feeling of being trapped in and enclosed grew more ominous. The air seemed strange in the large space without a view of the external world.

Elsa remained poised near the front of the dining hall. Bruce stood alongside her and whispered something to her, something that made her nod. Nancy hustled up to both of them and said, "I'm getting really worried about Carmella."

Elsa seemed like a frantic bird. "I don't know where she is."

"I tried to call her."

Elsa's tears rolled down her cheeks then. "This is the single most selfish thing she's ever done. She must know we're out of our minds with worry!"

"I don't think we should play the blame game just yet," Nancy told her. "We don't know the whole story."

"The only story right now is that a tropical storm is on its way, the island is in danger, and everyone needs to take cover," Elsa said pointedly.

Nancy tried again to dial Carmella, and again, the call went straight to voicemail. She hustled out into the parking lot, where three buses had lined themselves in expectation. Several Lodge guests had jumped onto the buses and now huddled near the windows, watching as the rain flashed across the glass. Nancy's hair dribbled down her shoulders.

Bruce appeared in a large raincoat. His eyes were frantic as he searched for Elsa. Elsa bounded down from one of the buses and flung her arms around him. "Are you sure you can't come with us?"

"I have to go get my family," he told her. "But I'll bring them to the safe house immediately afterward. I'll meet you there, I promise you."

Bruce kissed her and then hustled toward the far end of the parking lot, where he revved his engine and made his way out through the dark and sloshy roads. It was difficult to imagine, but Nancy had seen it before— miles and miles of Martha's Vineyard roads, covered only with water off the Nantucket Sound.

Janine appeared wearing a backpack and a large raincoat, with a hood wrapped over her forehead, allowing only her eyes to peer out. She gripped her mother's shoulder and said, "Let's get on the bus, okay? The Lodge is protected, and our guests are all on board. Time for us to hunker down."

But Nancy blared, "No!" far louder than she'd expected to. Janine's eyes widened, but Nancy soon explained. "We have to find Carmella. She isn't the kind of person to know what to do in these kinds of situations. She won't protect herself to the fullest because she doesn't feel she deserves protecting."

Janine's eyes hardened with understanding.

"You and Elsa should go with our guests," Nancy affirmed as she set her jaw. "But I'm going to drive over to Carmella's apartment and investigate."

"Her apartment is close to the waterline," Janine said hesitantly.

"I know." Nancy's heart pounded with worry. "But Janine, I can't go to the safe house knowing one of my girls is still out there. I owe it to Neal to keep his baby safe."

"But you owe it to me to keep yourself safe," Janine whispered. Then hurriedly, she added, "I know that's self-ish, but it's true."

Janine's eyes filled with tears. "Go. Get on the bus. Please."

Elsa appeared alongside Janine. Her hair had flattened over her neck and her forehead. "Get on the bus," she echoed. "Both of you. I heard a rumor the storm will soon transition to a hurricane."

"Oh God." Janine's face scrunched tighter. "Mom, seriously? You can't risk this."

"Risk what?" Elsa howled against the wind.

"I have to find Carmella!" Nancy called. She reached into her pocket to check that her keys remained. "If all goes according to plan, we'll be back on the road in no time."

Elsa's eyes darkened. "That's so dangerous, Nancy. So, so dangerous."

Nancy wanted to tell her just how little she currently cared about that. But she felt on the brink of death anyway; she could risk the little time she had left.

"I just can't let her go," Nancy whispered. "It's my fault she's out there on her own. She should be here with us."

Elsa and Janine exchanged glances. It seemed that a whole conversation hummed between their eyes.

"Get on the bus," Nancy insisted again. "Let's get going. We can't just stand out here until the hurricane whisks us away."

"We're going with you," Elsa blurted then.

"It's final," Janine affirmed.

"Girls. Seriously. No." Nancy shook her head so violently that her hair slapped her cheeks.

"Nancy. Don't be stupid. We're in this together," Elsa blared. She then jumped toward the front bus, where she spoke to one of the bus drivers and pointed toward the exit. In a moment, one by one, the buses eased out toward the road and then snaked up toward the inner belly of the island, where the Katama Lodge guests would be spared from the severity of the storm.

This just left Nancy, Elsa, and Janine in the parking lot, in the shadow of the huge Lodge— all at a loss and stirring in total fear. Nancy then gripped her car keys and flung them out of her pocket. "Let's go. Are you with me?"

They rushed toward Nancy's BMW— a gift from Neal a few years ago and nothing she felt she deserved. Nancy turned the keys in the ignition as Janine gathered herself in the passenger seat, and Elsa latched her seat belt in the back. The radio announcer seemed to have a lot to say, and none of it was good news.

"We've now fully transitioned from tropical storm to hurricane," he announced. "Batten down the hatches, islanders. Get to a safe place. Remember that just because we live in paradise doesn't mean that nature won't take its toll on all of us. Also, think of your neighbors and friends, anyone who might not have a place to go right now. Reach out to them. Call them if you can. Remember that often, the cell service goes out for hours or even days at a time."

"I wish she would answer her stupid phone!" Elsa cried from the back, having tried Carmella again.

"It's off," Nancy shot out. "Or maybe she lost it?"

"I don't know. Now that the guests are safe, my brain is bleeding with worry for my silly sister," Elsa continued.

The radio announcer had more to say. "And we're just getting news now that the hurricane has a name. And that name is Hurricane Janine."

Janine burst into laughter. She howled and placed her hand over her mouth. Nancy and Elsa joined in, both in shock.

"I wonder if God is playing some kind of trick on us?" Janine asked.

"It wouldn't be the first time," Elsa returned.

Nancy drove as swiftly as she could. Their tires slushed through growing puddles, and rain flattened its droplets against the windshield so rapidly that the wipers couldn't keep up. Nancy's fingers were bright white as she clutched the steering wheel.

"There. It's there." Elsa pounded the back of Janine's seat with her fists when she spotted Carmella's apartment building's sign, which was slightly crooked— proof this wasn't exactly a fine place to live. But, as far as Nancy knew, Carmella had never made a high income and had lived carefully, even as Elsa and Aiden had bought that mansion down the road and built their fortunes. For Carmella, a small apartment for one had always been enough.

The apartment building's parking lot was essentially a lake already. Nancy's tires laced through one side of it as she rushed toward Carmella's portion of the apartment complex. She parked near the tree line, then immediately leaped back into the torrential rain.

"Hurricane Janine!" she cried as she raced toward the staircase, which led up to Carmella's apartment. Unfortunately, her voice was lost to the whipping winds.

Janine and Elsa jumped up the steps behind her. In a moment, they hovered outside Carmella's door as Nancy's fist pounded at the wood. "CARMELLA? ARE YOU IN THERE?"

"It looks dark." Elsa peered through the window located left of the door. "She's not here."

At that moment, one of the enormous trees on the edge of the parking lot ripped up from the ground below, roots and all. The sound was monstrous as Janine, Nancy, and Elsa turned around just as the tree pounded across Nancy's BMW. Glass shards scattered; there was a horrible crunch. And in the moments that followed, the three Remington-Grimson women were far too petrified to do anything but stand there and listen to the howl of the wind.

Chapter Sixteen

It was almost comical. Maybe later, they would find ways to tell this story, highlighting just how stupid this all was. But just then, as the trees flattened with the severity of the wind and the parking lot grew deeper into a lake, the clouds darkened, and comedy was the furthest thing from their minds. Nancy, Elsa, and Janine hovered under the overhang at Carmella's apartment building with lackluster, frightened hearts. They were miles from the safe house. And when Nancy lifted her phone to call someone for help, they realized cell service was down. They were trapped.

In a rush, Elsa took off toward the far end of the apartment building and began to rap on people's doors, hollering for help. But everyone had retreated from the apartment building, knowing that it wasn't exactly a safe place to wait out the storm.

"We should have known Carmella was too smart to stay here," Elsa pointed out as she pressed her hands over her eyes. "Although with how down she gets, there was no telling what she would do."

Nancy kicked the side of the railing and again blinked down at her dilapidated BMW. Her stomach tightened with panic.

"Wouldn't she be with Cody, regardless?" she said suddenly.

Elsa dropped her hands from her eyes. "Yes, of course."

"And do you have any idea of where he lives?"

Elsa pressed her lips into a line and pondered. Janine stepped toward the staircase; with her hood so tight over her head, she looked like an alien, the first to explore the earth and all its wild climates. "We should get to the road regardless before the water rises."

Nancy followed Janine as Elsa continued to think about Cody's location. The water had already lined itself around the bottom of the staircase; Nancy dreaded to see what sort of havoc the water would take on these bottom floors. She'd seen flood footage before with families wading in through their old residences, up to their waists in water as they looked at their old wardrobes and blackened televisions.

She prayed the mansion on the south side would be spared.

But of course, if the house went with the storm, then it went with the storm. All she truly cared about was her girls, her family. All her life, she had lost things, people, situations, and residences. She knew what mattered most now. She had enough experience to know.

Martha's Vineyard no longer felt like Martha's Vineyard. It was now akin to a war zone. The rain splattered across their heads as they sloshed through the edges of the massive puddle and headed up the small hill toward the main road. Nobody spoke. There was nothing to say, and the wind was far too loud for anyone to be heard. With each step, Nancy fell deeper into feelings of guilt. She should have forced the girls to get on the buses. Maybe she should have gotten on a bus herself.

It's just that she wouldn't have forgiven herself if something had happened to Carmella.

When they reached the main road, Elsa pointed toward the right. "If I'm not mistaken, Cody lives this way."

"How far is the walk?" Janine hollered.

"I don't know." Elsa bit hard on her lower lip again and glanced leftward. "I can't remember the last time I saw this road empty. It's like a ghost town."

They staggered along for a few minutes. Nancy continued to glance back, checking for some sign of a vehicle— anyone who could help them. Janine took her hood off her head and said she was soaked through, regardless. "The best quality raincoat has nothing on Hurricane Janine," she blurted out.

Nancy's throat tightened. She glanced back yet again and caught sight of a truck. It was a crooked, busted-up truck, one that had seen much better days. It plugged along through the winds and rain, and before she knew what she'd done, Nancy swung out into the center of the road, trying to wave the vehicle down.

"Mom! What are you doing?" Janine cried.

But Nancy knew all too well she had to flag this truck down if they wanted to get anywhere. This wasn't any worse than the hitchhiking she'd done all over the United States, across Europe, and into Asia, during those years after she'd left New York and prior to her move to Martha's Vineyard. It was funny how she could drop back into this mindset so easily, especially in times of strife.

The truck halted just a few feet away. The rain was so heavy; they couldn't make out who was in the driver's seat.

"What if he's a murderer?" Elsa whispered as they rushed for the door.

"We can outsmart him, but we can't outsmart a hurricane," Nancy told her, just before she yanked open the passenger side for a full view of the inside of the truck.

There, seated in the driver's seat, was a man in his late sixties, early seventies. Nancy had met him only a handful of times over the years, as he tended to spend time alone. As a result, he was dubbed one of the island's recluses.

His name was Stan Ellis. And he was something of a pariah around Martha's Vineyard. He'd been on the boat that had sunk the night Anna Sheridan had died. He'd been driving it without the lights on, and she'd been cheating on her husband, Wes. As a result, he'd destroyed a family.

And Nancy knew the guilt had nearly destroyed him. You could see it in the wrinkles etched across his face and the hollowness of his eyes.

"Get in," he ordered, waving them in with his arm.

They did as they were told. Elsa and Janine hopped into the smaller back seat, still within the confines of the truck's enclosed space. Nancy took the front seat and latched her seat belt.

"What are you girls doing out here like this? You know you need to take cover." Stan's windshield wipers barely did anything against the rain. His eyes were petrified.

"I should say the same to you," Nancy told him. "We

have to check on my daughter, Carmella. We're worried she's not safe."

Stan's face loosened slightly. "Do you know where she is?"

"We have a hunch," Nancy replied.

Stan nodded. "But if she's not there, there's no time to run around the island looking for her. We don't have long before this hurricane goes full-blast on us. I've seen it happen before."

He slammed his foot on the gas, and the busted truck moved forward. The radio was nothing but white noise. Stan seemed not to notice and made no adjustment.

"But where are you going to take shelter?" Janine finally asked from the back.

Stan arched an eyebrow. He grunted, then said, "Just tell me where to turn off."

Nobody spoke for another few minutes. The experience felt like going to the car wash— pushing your car through a sort of torrential nightmare. The world was that nightmare, and there was no reprieve at the other end.

"Here. I think it's here," Elsa said, pointing at a little driveway.

Cody's house was nothing to write home about. He had probably just as many pennies to rub together as Carmella, and already, the waterline had rushed toward the backyard and rippled around the fence. And toward the left of that fence was a familiar, beautiful sight.

Carmella had parked her car there.

"She must be here!" Elsa cried.

Stan parked the truck at the far end of the driveway, only ten or so feet in front of the encroaching waterline. He kept the motor running, explaining that sometimes when he turned off the engine, it took a while to start back up again.

"Not a good time to tell us that," Janine said as she jumped out from the truck and headed for Cody's door.

Nancy and Elsa rushed behind her. Nancy's hair ripped behind her as she staggered through the growing puddles. She prayed with everything she had that Carmella was there.

Janine pounded her fist over and over again as Elsa and Nancy howled Carmella and Cody's names. They sounded half drunk and half out of their minds. Janine's pounds grew more chaotic. Finally, Elsa suggested that probably, Cody and Carmella had taken refuge in one of the inner rooms and attributed every noise to the sound of the storm outside.

"How can we sound different?" Janine cried.

Nancy noticed a bell. The bell seemed to have been hung on the porch, a little trinket from a previous era; probably, Carmella or Cody had removed it when the winds had begun and placed it off to the side. It was quite heavy, probably nothing that could be whipped away with the storm.

Now, Nancy lifted the bell and began to jingle it as loudly as she could. Each jangle of the bell took so much from her; she felt her strength depleting as she thrust it forward and back again.

Meanwhile, Janine banged away at the door as Elsa screamed. They were the worst kind of girl band.

"Please," Nancy breathed, her voice growing lost to the storm. "Please. Hear us."

Finally, the door slowly opened to reveal Cody. He looked frightened and perturbed all at once. Then when he realized who was on his porch, he whipped open the door still wider and hollered back toward Carmella, who held Cody's three-year-old, Gretchen, across her chest and over her shoulder.

"It's your family!"

Nancy's heart shattered at the sight of Carmella. She hadn't seen her since she'd stormed away that night. Now, Nancy realized the stupidity of what had happened. How childish she'd been, even at fifty-nine years old.

"Carmella!" Nancy tore past Cody and headed straight for her darling stepdaughter. She placed a tender hand over Gretchen's curly hair and wrapped her other arm around Carmella, holding on to her as the house threatened to fall apart. "I was so worried about you. So, so worried."

When Nancy stepped back, Carmella's eyes were filled with tears. She adjusted Gretchen across her shoulder as her cheeks brightened to pink.

"I don't know what to say," she whispered.

"You don't have to say anything. I was out of line, and I'm so sorry," Nancy tried to apologize. "Whatever happens next, I want us all to be together in everything. No secrets. And no hiding away!"

Gretchen howled again as tears spilled from her eyes. Cody bucked back from the front door and said, "We have to get back in the bathroom. It's the safest place."

"We have that safe house," Nancy told him. "And Stan has offered to drive us up. But we only have a little more time, and the water outside this house is threatening to rise even higher. I'm not convinced it will hold."

Cody and Carmella locked eyes. You could feel the immensity of their love for one another, something they'd only just recently acknowledged.

"We have to go," Carmella said softly. "The storm

could go on for hours. This house might not make it."

Cody's face was stern. He ran a strong hand through his hair and then rubbed the back of his neck, contemplating their next move. "Okay. Okay. Is the truck big enough?"

"It will have to be," Janine said. "Let's go."

They re-entered the exterior hall and rushed back toward Stan Ellis through the rain. Carmella looked at the older man with disbelief. She only really knew him as "Anna Sheridan's murderer," or whatever it was people called him even though they didn't know the entire story. But right then, he was their ticket to freedom.

Cody and Carmella sat tightly together toward the left of the back seat. Gretchen wrapped herself around Carmella like a monkey to a tree. Nancy piled in alongside them while Janine and Elsa shared the passenger seat.

"Everyone, hold on tight!" Stan hollered as though he was the patriarch in a large family, and these words were typical for him.

While staring at him, Nancy thought to herself, had he ever wanted to build a family with Anna Sheridan? Had he wanted the sort of love the Sheridans had?

For the first time, Nancy drew comparisons to her previous self and this current version of Stan Ellis. Had she not met Neal, she would have been just as alone and sad as the man before them.

"Let's get to safety," Stan said as he made it out toward the main road and headed away from the torrential seas. "Nothing out here for us now. Sometimes I tell myself I'll move to the plains— Kansas or something like that. I don't know that the ocean has ever been particularly kind to me."

Chapter Seventeen

F ar down the road, they encountered another uprooted tree. It had stripped itself across the full span of the road, completely splayed out, blocking everything in its path. Rivers from the Bay now swam around it as Stan hovered his truck about fifteen feet from the wreck. He muttered to himself, then steered the truck back quickly. "We have to find another way."

Nancy's heart pounded wildly in her throat. The clouds were thicker, monstrously dark, and hovering so close to the treetops. As the truck moved back down the road, one of the tires dropped into an enormous pothole, and Carmella nearly lost her grip on Gretchen. Gretchen flung up slightly from her lap before Carmella could fully latch her down again. Frightened, Gretchen began to wail. The sound filled the tight space in the truck. Stan muttered even more, louder and more aggressively, mostly to himself.

"Shhh, Gretch. It's okay." Carmella's words were tender yet edged with her sorrow and pain. She splayed her hand over Gretchen's hair and stroked it as her eyes grew wider.

"It's okay, Bean," Cody breathed to his daughter. "You're just scared, but you're not hurt. See? Carmella has you safe. We have you safe."

But Gretchen wasn't convinced, not completely. She wailed again and clenched her eyes shut. Nancy placed her hand on Gretchen's back and smoothed down her little dress, which was ruffled up in the back from all the chaos.

"It's okay, Gretchen. Really."

Even against the howl of the wind, the sound of someone else's voice was surprising to Gretchen. She turned to find Nancy's eyes and furrowed her eyebrows almost angrily, as though she couldn't believe someone else, someone she hardly knew, was in her space.

"Hi, Gretchen. You remember me, right? You've been to my house before." Nancy spoke gently with the slightest of smiles. "Do you know that your friend Carmella is my stepdaughter?"

Gretchen shook her head as hard as she could, but she didn't turn away from Nancy. Instead, her eyes tore into Nancy's as though she tried to read the language of her soul.

"That's right. She's my stepdaughter, and I love her very, very much," Nancy said.

Carmella's face was difficult to read. It had loosened a lot since they'd discovered them at Cody's house; her eyes shone with tears that she still refused to let fall.

"I love her so much, and I hope she knows that I would never stay mad at her. No matter what," Nancy continued to say, directing the words to Gretchen.

Stan drove the truck back down another side road,

switched gears, and then flung them up a hill, farther and farther from the growing rivers and streams and puddles-turned-lakes. He whipped his head back and whistled. "That's right, Hurricane Janine. You won't take us. Not today!"

Carmella's smile broke out in disbelief then. "They named it Hurricane Janine?"

"That's right. What a year, huh? Maybe my ex-husband knows the guy in charge of that," Janine said from the front seat.

Carmella cackled. "That would be a new blow, wouldn't it?"

"Come on. You saw Jack Potter at Maggie's wedding. He's capable of evil things," Elsa said.

"Unfortunately, that's very true," Janine breathed. "I only just realized recently how abusive that marriage was."

Carmella adjusted Gretchen against her chest. "Here's to all the years of therapy we need for all the people who wronged us in our lives. Like Karen and Jack, and all the others."

"Here's to that," Janine affirmed with a crooked smile.

Nancy's heart darkened just a little. After all, wasn't she one of those people who'd wronged Janine so greatly? But then again, this was what humans did to other humans: they hurt one another, even in their love. "We're all a collection of emotions, feelings, and beliefs— and we try to throw ourselves together in love and harmony and don't always make the best of it." Nancy had written this once in her diary when she had tried to digest her faults in Janine's life.

Nancy kept her hand splayed on Gretchen's back,

helping to calm her as they whizzed toward the safe house. Elsa gave Stan directions as they went, saying over and over again, "Not long now. We're almost there." It was calming to hear her say this. Finally, all of the trauma of the past thirty-or-so minutes would remain in the past. Finally, they'd made it through.

Nancy lifted her eyes toward Carmella's and said, "I don't mind that you told. I shouldn't have kept it a secret, anyway."

Carmella's chin quivered. "I am so sorry for wronging you like that."

"No. Listen to me, Carmella. It was a stupid thing to get so angry about. I'm just frightened about all of it, but that's no reason to take out that emotion on you. I want you in my life, Carmella. I want our friendship to be stronger than ever, but what I want most is our mother-daughter relationship with all its complexities. That's what I want. And I think we can get there if you want to try. Do you?"

Carmella nodded. She looked to be deep inside her head, her thoughts stirring far beyond her eyes.

But finally, she nodded as a tear rolled down her cheek. Then she spoke. "I want that, too. I want trust between us. I want to build something with you. And I think we're capable of it."

Nancy draped her head against Carmella's shoulder and tenderly traced her hand down Gretchen's back. Her heart felt too big for her chest, like the Grinch who stole Christmas.

Stan yanked the truck into the lot at the safe house. Then finally, they all popped out of the truck and inhaled the fresh yet rain-filled air around them. Bruce stood at the doorway, completely drenched, and hollered for Elsa.

She rushed into his arms as he said, "You weren't answering any of my calls, and then the service ran out, and I just—" He shook his head menacingly, even as relief fell over his face.

Their large group was like a mass of wet rats, ducking into a clean and safe space. Their hair whipped around, drenched, and their skin was sallow and pale from the chill. Down the long hallway, a few of the guests from the Katama Lodge caught sight of them and whispered to one another, skeptical. Nancy couldn't care.

They were safe. That was all that mattered.

On the left wall of the foyer area, Neal had hung one of their wedding photographs. In it, Neal whispered something into Nancy's ear as Nancy laughed wildly, her hand draped over her stomach. Nancy would have paid maybe a million dollars to know what Neal had said at that moment. Why couldn't she remember? It seemed so perfect now. She was so envious of that other Nancy.

"Janine!" Henry rushed out from the main belly of the safe house.

"Henry! I'm so glad you finally listened to me," Janine said. She threw her arms around him as well and nuzzled her head against his chest.

"Of course. Well, I managed to get a few great hurricane shots, but imagine my surprise when I arrived here much later than even I expected, and you weren't here yet," Henry told her with a slight tone of sarcasm.

Janine buzzed her lips. "We had an adventure. Do you know Stan? He saved our lives."

Henry was an islander, so naturally, he'd heard the tales of Stan Ellis over the years. Now, though, he stretched out his hand and shook Stan's firmly.

"Thank you for bringing Janine up here. I can't

imagine what kind of trouble she was in."

"Caught the three of them flagging me down from the side of the road," Stan affirmed with a cheeky grin.

"You don't say? Teaching them some of your tricks, Nancy?" Henry asked.

Nancy winked at him, then gathered her hair back behind her head and stepped toward where the staff and women of Katama Lodge had created a unique space to wait out the storm. A battery-powered stereo system had been plugged in, and soft tunes swirled overhead, creating an ambiance of peace and serenity.

The staff members had gotten to work. They poured wine, passed around snacks, and set up couches and mattresses with blankets and pillows. They greeted the guests warmly and asked them their comfort levels as the women fell into these same pillows, turned to one another, and began to gossip and dream.

There was such a contrast between this space and the one outside. It nearly gave Nancy whiplash.

Toward the far end of the room, she collapsed on a red couch. One of the staff members almost immediately delivered her a glass of wine and asked if she needed anything else. "A towel, maybe?"

Nancy laughed dryly. "I feel too exhausted to do anything but sit here and drink this, I'm afraid."

Janine, Elsa, and Carmella stepped out from the foyer. Cody held Gretchen and bobbed her around as she slept. He conversed with Bruce and Henry, men who had fast become his friends. As Elsa, Carmella, and Janine neared Nancy, the same staff member approached with glasses of wine. Mallory also stepped out from the bathroom, baby Zachery in her arms, and greeted her mother warmly.

"Cole and I got here a little while ago," she told her mother. "We were terrified when we figured out you weren't here."

Elsa exhaled and sipped her wine. "We made it. What about Lucas?"

"He's here. We broke up last night but then got back together a few minutes ago," Mallory said with a bright, silly smile. "I don't know what to do about it. I can't get rid of my love for him."

Elsa slid a tender hand down her daughter's shoulder. "Love is complicated, isn't it?"

"The most complicated and beautiful thing of all," Mallory agreed.

Carmella and Janine sat on either side of Nancy on the couch. Soon after, Elsa joined them. They sat in silence for a moment, all of them drying out yet still slick. Soon, they would have to find dry clothes; soon, they would move forward from this peace. But just then, they had to roll through this strange and nuanced emotion.

They'd all just lived through something enormous. Perhaps it was so big that it didn't even deserve words.

"I love you three," Nancy finally offered. "My daughter and my two stepdaughters. I feel more grateful than I can say that I have you in my life. I have made almost every single mistake. I honestly don't deserve you."

"We've all made mistakes," Elsa insisted.

"Well, I have," Carmella said with a laugh.

"Let's not point fingers. Not at ourselves or one another," Janine said.

"Maybe we should make a pact," Nancy suggested, looking from one to the next. "Not to blame and to do everything, going forward, with love and empathy."

Janine placed her hand in the air between all of them.

One by one, like a sports team, they placed their hands over Janine's, then counted to three and whipped their hands in the air, giggling. Several of the Katama Lodge guests glanced their way, confused, before turning back to their wine and snacks.

Sometimes when Nancy peered into these women's eyes, she wanted to tell them just how little money she'd had until only about a decade before. She wondered what these judgmental women would make of her if they'd only known that really, she had been something of a beggar in New York City— sometimes selling purses on the side of the road.

Life was so varied. You never knew what would happen next.

But you had to have belief in the power of change. Nancy knew that.

"I wonder how long we'll be in here," Janine said thoughtfully.

"Sometimes these storms last for twenty-four hours," Elsa breathed.

"I guess we'd better think of something to do with all these women," Nancy said.

"You don't think wine and conversation will be enough for them?" Carmella asked.

Nancy considered this. She watched as the women's conversations grew more and more intense, as their wine-glasses were filled, as the air overhead seemed wildly provocative and charged with some kind of hope. In a sense, it was the perfect ecosystem for these women, as they were women who'd come from all states and all walks of life— if only to commune with women just a little bit lost, like them.

Chapter Eighteen

There was an ever-present sense of danger. The air was sinister, even as women gossiped and laughed into the night. They clutched their wineglasses with tense fingers and glanced toward the far door, which was latched tight and overly thick against the winds and rain. Around eight, several of the staff members gathered in the kitchen area and began to make a multi-course meal out of the supplies the safe house had been stocked with, plus the vegetables and fruits and dairy they'd brought over from the Katama Lodge itself. Anxious, Nancy walked through the kitchen and listened to the bright and orchestrated language between the chef and her kitchen staff members. Regardless of the state of the world or how close they were to the end of it, people needed to eat, and the chef wanted to ensure that this meal was unlike any other.

Nancy again checked her phone for any sign of the state of things outside. This was a stupid move; after all, the weather had only ramped up since their mad dash into the safe house. It would probably be another few days before the internet service returned.

It was strange, being at the safe house like this. In a way, Nancy was grateful, as she knew all the people she loved most in the world were right there, between those walls (besides Alyssa and Maggie, who were both safe from this hurricane, at least). Still, it was isolating to be away from all the other islanders, all of whom were probably latched away in similar hiding places, praying for the end of the hurricane.

Once, just after Nancy had met Neal in Thailand, she'd asked him about tropical storms and if they'd ever had their way with Martha's Vineyard. His eyes had grown shadowed. "It's difficult to remember them after they happen. I think that's how a lot of trauma is. You hunker down and get through it, and then after, you can hardly believe it was you who had the clarity of thought to save yourself and others. I don't know if you know what I mean." Nancy had nodded, tears in her eyes, and explained that she knew far more than she could even let on. Hadn't most everything in her life, pre-Neal, been a sort of a storm?

The meal was immaculate, something oddly magical in the midst of so much strife. More Lodge staff members set up long tables and placed them with glowing plates, bright silverware, wine and water glasses. Nancy hovered near the doorway between the kitchen and the larger room until finally Elsa came and dragged her to the table to sit alongside the rest of them. "You're going to tire yourself out," Elsa scolded. "Come on."

Just beneath the bustling conversation and the clinking of the silverware, if you listened, really listened, you could make out the ravenous howling of the winds from Hurricane Janine. Nancy furrowed her brow as she latched onto that sound, her fork raised over her plate. Janine splayed her hand over Nancy's elbow and whispered, "I hear it, too."

"It sounds just awful out there," Nancy said under her breath.

"But we're in here. We're safe," Janine returned. "Don't focus on anything else."

Nancy nodded as fear continued to wrap around her heart and drag it down. She scrunched her nose the slightest bit, then added, "I just wish Neal was here. He always knew what to do."

Janine, who'd never met Neal, nodded, furrowing her brow. "But you've done everything right. I know you wish he was here. I know you love him with all your heart. But we don't need him to keep these women safe. We've done everything we can."

After a pumpkin-cream soup, Lodge staff members whisked the bowls away and returned with salads, fresh with plump tomatoes and vibrant spinach greens and walnuts and gorgonzola. Nancy was surprised to feel her appetite returning.

Off to her right, Bruce and Elsa sat side by side, their shoulders touching. Bruce murmured into Elsa's ear, and Elsa nodded and gave him a playful, half-secret smile. Beside Janine, Henry sat and described more of the shots he'd taken for the documentary— a project that seemed never-ending, at least in Nancy's eyes. She had met several "New York City artist types" when she'd lived in Brooklyn, and they had always had a project to discuss, much like Henry. The difference with him, of course, was that he had a good heart and left his arrogance at the door. That was essential.

The main course was a rich barbecue chicken with herb-crusted potatoes. Some of the women at the table murmured that they hadn't had anything so "sinful" in over five years. One turned and spoke directly to Janine, her head doctor, and asked if this sort of meal wouldn't knock back her health plan for several months.

Janine gave the woman a crooked smile. "Well, to be honest with you, I believe in moderation above all things. And today, as the world rages outside, I think we can take a moment to fuel ourselves, nourish our minds, and relax about silly things like food rules."

The woman's eyes widened with surprise. Soon after, she tore into her barbecue chicken with a large appetite, then joined into whatever gossip swirled around her, beaming with life.

Just before a honey-based dessert was served, Nancy stood and clicked her fork against her glass gently, just loud enough so that the women turned their attention toward her. They knew Nancy as the owner of the Lodge, the woman whose husband had started the movement. Their eyes glittered with respect.

"Good evening, everyone. Thank you for being so responsible and kind in the midst of so much havoc. We can say it over and over again, but it's true every time: we can't control the weather. I wish we could. If I had it my way, we'd all be at the beach right now, sipping mimosas and doing yoga. But alas! We're here in this safe house, which my husband, Neal, arranged for the women at the Lodge. I am so grateful for his foresight. I feel him with us here and now watching over us, making sure we're in good spirits, fed and safe.

"Since we're all trapped in here together for the foreseeable future— at least until tomorrow and maybe into the next day, depending on the state of things outside ..."

At this, several of the women yanked their heads around to one another and muttered with alarm. Again, Nancy clinked her fork against her glass.

"Don't worry, everyone. Really. I promise you. Where we are now is the safest place on the island. We will consider the state of things hour by hour and ensure you a safe journey, either to another place on the island or off the island and back home again. This will all seem like a bad dream.

"But in the meantime, I'd like to ask us all to do a little experiment before dessert. I'd like everyone to stand and say something they're grateful for, here and now, while the world shifts and turns with the chaos outside. I think it's essential for us to remind ourselves of what we love and what we need, and how incredible our lives are. It's a part of our practice at the Katama Lodge, and I'd like to bring it here, to the Katama Lodge's safe house."

There was silence at the table. All eyes continued to blink up at Nancy, incredulous. After a pause, Nancy gave them a soft smile. "Okay. I can kick things off. I don't mind." She swallowed, then procceded. "Many of you probably don't know my backstory. You know me as Neal's wife— a woman who has supported him in all things at the Lodge for the previous twelve or so years. Naturally, my life took a very sharp turn in January of this year when Neal passed away. I was devastated to lose him. If I'm honest, I sometimes miss him so much, my stomach hurts. None of you are strangers to loss. I've been in conversation with many of you since you arrived at the Lodge. I've heard your stories and your heartaches. It's something we, as women and as people, all share. Sorrow is something that stitches us all together.

"But what many of you don't know about me is that I wasn't always Nancy Remington, Neal's wife. I met Neal rather late in my journey. Prior to that, I was something of a vagabond. I traveled across the world with very little money, sleeping in slum hostels and bad hotels and on people's couches. People used and abused me over the years, and I never thought I deserved anything better than what I had.

"I don't mean to complain. I mean only to illustrate just how grateful I am, now, for what I have. Neal Remington showed me that I am worthy of so much more than my past. But beyond that, I want to say that I'm grateful for that past because it shaped me into who I am today. It made me braver than I ever thought possible. And maybe I needed every single one of those hard days, if only so it led me to some of the most beautiful ones of my life.

"I also want to say just how grateful I am for my family. No matter what happens next, the fact that I have my Janine and my Elsa and my Carmella here with me means the world." Nancy lifted her wineglass toward each of the women around her as her eyes filled with tears. Outside, the wind thrust itself against the safe house, and a shiver ran down Nancy's spine.

"Okay. Who's next?" Nancy said with a funny laugh as she swiped a tear from beneath her eye. "I think that's enough blubbering from this old lady."

In the wake of her speech, several women stood to preach their gratefulness.

Janine stood to say how grateful she was for her newfound relationship with her mother and her daughter's recent marriage to the love of her life. "It's strange to realize that the children you brought into this world have the strength and power to go off on their own and make these huge, life-altering decisions. But my Maggie has this way about her. She doesn't even glance back with a hint of regret."

Elsa's gratefulness extended over her daughters, Alexie and Mallory, her son, Cole, her sister, Carmella, her father, Neal, her stepmother, Nancy, and her newfound stepsister, Janine. "I lost my husband last year, and I thought I might never be happy again. It just goes to show you that optimism is one of the greatest things you can harness to change your own life. I never want to forget that again."

After Carmella and Mallory said their own words of gratefulness, several women from the crowd took their opportunities, as well.

"I'm grateful for the mindfulness and meditation I've used for my healing here at the Katama Lodge and Wellness Spa," one woman in her forties said softly, her voice meek. "In the real world, I'm always so frantic and outside of myself. But here on Martha's Vineyard, I've found a way back to my own mind."

Another woman explained her gratefulness for Carmella's acupuncturist clinic, which had aided in her anxiety symptoms over the span of several sessions. Another said she was grateful for her mother, who'd recently passed away but left her a wonderful sense of adventure and curiosity. Another said she was grateful for her body, which, even into her fifties, allowed her to go on long runs, upward of thirteen miles. "My grandchildren can't keep up with me," she said with a funny smile. "I know one day, my body will give out on me. But I hope that day is a long, long time from now."

When everyone returned to their seats, the dessert was served. Nancy's heart swelled with the stories of all these women, whose gratefulness brewed over them, thickening like the storm clouds above. Janine placed a hand over Nancy's and squeezed gently.

"You know how to make people think," she said.

Nancy gave a light shrug. "It's because I didn't know how to think for so long. I had to train myself. And it completely changed my life."

Janine's eyes filled with tears. "It's changing mine, too."

Chapter Nineteen

P hone service returned to the island the following morning just before six. Nancy stretched her legs out beneath the comforter until her toes crept up into the air as she braced herself for news of the outside world. The frantic howling of the wind had died out somewhere around two or three in the morning, at which time Bruce and Henry had stepped out to assess the exterior world. As they were located on higher ground, and the streets remained black and wicked, Nancy and the other girls had insisted they return to the safe house until morning. "We can't do anything now," Janine had said firmly.

Unfortunately, there wasn't a whole lot of information yet about the state of Martha's Vineyard. Nobody had had social media to report anything; everyone had existed solely within their own storylines, unable to compare. Nancy's heart beat wildly as she considered the hours ahead. She prayed that no horrible stories would come out of this time; she prayed that the island had made it through the night.

Unable to sleep a wink longer, she placed her feet on the floor alongside the bed and gazed out through the darkness. Her bed was located in one of the smaller rooms, which was attached to the main room. In this room were three other beds, where Bruce, Elsa, Janine, Henry, Carmella, and Cody all slept. Mallory, Lucas, and Zachery were in a smaller room down the hall, set aside for them because Zachery hadn't stopped crying when he started around midnight. Gretchen had passed out on her father's chest around nine in the evening, and he'd placed her delicately in a larger crib, one that Nancy was surprised to find in one of the back closets. Apparently, Neal had thought of everything as he'd arranged the space.

Nancy stood in the kitchen as coffee bubbled and spat into the pot. She rubbed her eyes and then began to scribe a list of essential tasks for the day ahead. Namely, she had to figure out how to get these women either back home or back to the Lodge— whatever the Lodge allowed and whatever the women willed. Beyond that, she had to arm her heart for what awaited her at the Lodge. If there was a great deal of damage, she couldn't let it harm her. "One day at a time," she whispered to herself now. They could handle whatever was thrown at them.

Family drama and hurricanes and potentially life-threatening diseases— it all offered a unique balancing act that very well could make her go crazy.

But she wouldn't go crazy. Not today.

As she poured her first cup of coffee, someone entered the kitchen. She flashed her eyes up to find none other than Stan Ellis. He looked run down, and his knees seemed to bend awkwardly as he walked toward her. His eyes remained far away even as he tried out a soft, shy smile. Throughout dinner the night before, he'd hardly said a peep, and when it was his turn to express his gratefulness, he'd lifted a glass and just said, "I'm grateful to be safe and surrounded by all you fine people." It had been enough, but of course, it hadn't been the full story. Not in the slightest.

Probably, Stan Ellis didn't have so much to be grateful for. It had been a hard road.

"Morning," he said. His voice was gritty and deep. His eyes, however, were earnest and bright. Nancy had a funny sensation, looking at him now. She could see the man he'd been some thirty years before, the man Anna Sheridan had fallen head-over-heels for. He'd been handsome; in a way, he still was.

"Good morning. Would you like a cup of coffee?"

"Sure would." He watched as Nancy poured him a mug and then thanked her.

"I hope you slept okay?"

"As well as I could," Stan told her. "In truth, I can't remember the last time I slept through the night."

Nancy's heart cracked the slightest bit. "I hate hearing that. Sleep is so important."

Stan shrugged. "I got used to it. Just a bit weird to be in a big room with so many other folks." He sipped his coffee, then nodded. "Funny to drink coffee in the morning after a disaster, isn't it? Life just keeps going forward, and you always need coffee to make it so."

Nancy marveled at his words. They seemed stitched into the back of her mind. She'd had a similar thought when Neal had passed away— that she couldn't believe she still needed to eat, to drink coffee, and to walk. How could these processes continue when so much had faltered?

Probably, Stan had felt the same when he'd lost Anna.

"Thank you again for letting me sleep here," Stan told her.

"Where were you headed when you stopped for us?"

Stan tilted his head. "I wasn't so sure. I just knew my little shack didn't have the will to withstand the storm."

"You were going to just sit in your truck?"

"Somewhere away from the water. Yeah."

Nancy shuddered to think what might have happened. She now shuddered to imagine the state of his shack. Assuredly, he needed a place to sleep that night, too.

Probably, he didn't have much money, either.

"I don't suppose you'd like to drive me down to the Lodge this morning," Nancy said suddenly. "I want to see the state of it before we plan out what to do with our guests."

"It would be my pleasure," Stan told her. "It's not like I have anything else going on."

Nancy gathered her purse, changed into her previous day's outfit, took a glance at herself in the mirror, then wrote a little note and placed it next to Janine's bed. It was just six thirty, and already, she and Stan strode out into the parking lot of the safe house as the sunlight swept across the tumultuous state of the island. Around the parking lot, several trees had fallen with the strength of the wind, casting themselves across the edge of the pavement and making it crackle beneath them. Stan whistled as he unlocked the truck.

"I guess I'd better mentally prepare for what state the rest of the island is in," he commented. "It's a strange sensation. When the island is attacked, I feel personally attacked. I'm no original islander, but I guess I've been here long enough that I ought to feel like one."

As they drove away from the safe house, something occurred to Nancy. "Isn't your stepson on the island?"

Stan nodded. "He normally lives on the island with that Lola Sheridan. Sweet girl."

"But he's not here now?"

"No." His face grew tense with a sudden wave of worry. "I just pray he wasn't out on the water."

Tommy Gasbarro was Stan Ellis's ex-stepson from a previous marriage. He was a very accomplished sailor and frequently won the Round the Island race, held every summer on the Vineyard. His sailing accomplishments had been the topic of one of Lola Sheridan's articles for a local Boston newspaper. She'd journeyed with him by boat from Florida all the way back to the Vineyard. Unfortunately, a storm had overtaken them in the midst of their expedition, and their boat had almost capsized.

It was their origin story— the reason, maybe, they'd fallen in love.

"If there's anybody who understands the intricacies of the ocean, it's Tommy Gasbarro," Nancy said softly. "I'm sure he's fine."

They continued their trek from the center of the island back toward Edgartown. The hurricane had eaten its way through trees and across fields. They'd witnessed several little houses, cracked along the side or with tree limbs bursting through their windows as though trying to perform some kind of heinous surgery. When they reached downtown, they had to backtrack to avoid wild rivers of flooding, which looked like it had impacted the local high school and some of the downtown restaurants and shops.

When they reached the Katama Lodge, Nancy stepped out of the truck a split second before Stan stopped the engine. When she hustled to the top of the hill that overlooked the Bay, she found that the water line had rushed toward the base of the Lodge itself; it had risen halfway up the various cabins down below, eating away at the furniture and the hardwood and the hand-selected décor.

But still— the waterline had stopped before any colossal damage to the greater Lodge. Nancy had to be grateful.

She then headed into the Lodge itself, which had been protected beautifully. Even the large window in the dining hall was fully intact. Stan entered and helped her move aside the large protective walls, which allowed the glorious glow of a fresh day to billow across the dining hall. Nancy's heart lifted with hope. It felt exactly like the days after the Great Flood when the dove appeared to Noah, and he knew, soon, there would be new life ahead.

"Stan," Nancy said as he gazed out across the Bay, which bubbled just below the edge of the large Lodge. "I want you to pick out a room for yourself and stay as long as you like until you can figure out what to do about your place."

Stan furrowed his brow. "I don't know what to say."

"Don't say anything. Just drive over to your place and get as much of your stuff as you can. Anything that made it through. We'd love to have you with open arms."

Stan nodded. He cupped his hands over his chest and said, "Thank you so much." He then swallowed and added, "What you said about being grateful after losing so much resonated with me. I don't know if I'll ever have the strength to build something again. But I do have so much, even after so much loss. I have to be grateful. Thank you again, Nancy."

Nancy gave him a genuine smile. "I think gratefulness is a superpower. If you can harness it, there's not a whole lot you can't have because you'll feel like you have everything you need."

Chapter Twenty

Henry was in full documentarian mode. He flashed his finger forward to alert her he'd pressed play. Nancy shifted her weight, then clasped and unclasped her hands due to her nerves. She stood just a few feet from where the water remained, a flooded lake over the docks around two feet high that still lingered around the surrounding cabins. Henry wanted to capture the intricate stories of Hurricane Janine; he wanted to weave them together in a way that allowed the island to heal and represent all voices, all those affected. As Nancy was his girlfriend's mother, he'd opted for Nancy first.

"What do you want me to say?" she asked him now, suddenly flummoxed.

"Just talk about what happened when the hurricane came and about the damage to the Lodge," Henry explained with the slightest hint of exasperation.

"Right. Okay." She cleared her throat. "When we heard about the approaching tropical storm, we knew we needed to get all of our guests to safety. Luckily, Neal, my husband, crafted a plan for such an event, and we took all the women of the Lodge up to higher ground. As you can see, the flooding from Hurricane Janine crept up over the waterline and flooded out several of our luxury cabins. Luckily for us, the main Lodge is intact and ready for operation again. Most of the women who'd been staying with us during the hurricane left the island yesterday, but we will begin to welcome new guests as early as next weekend."

Henry snapped his thumbs in affirmation and then asked, "What do you say to those more affected by the hurricane across the island?"

Nancy bowed her head somberly. "My heart goes out to those affected. The Hesson House, in particular, took a real blow. Olivia Hesson built a beautiful space out of that old mansion. It would be a real disservice to the island's culture as a whole if the mansion wasn't rebuilt."

Nancy watched from the parking lot as Henry weaved around the grounds, taking shots of the water and the flooded cabins below. She felt anxious and strange, as though her skin didn't quite fit her face. When Henry returned to the lot, he asked if she wanted to see some of the footage. She said no. She'd seen enough.

Back at the main house, which had mercifully been spared in the hurricane, Nancy found her three girls plus Mallory out on the back porch. It was a chilly day in late September, and they wore thick-knit sweaters and sipped hot tea. Nancy collapsed in her familiar chair and explained the events of the day, from having her car finally towed, to running into a strained Olivia Hesson downtown, to calling Wes Sheridan to see how the Sunrise Cove had made it through (generally unscathed, although the Bistro had taken a hit), to the final filming with Henry.

"Sounds like an exhausting day," Janine breathed.

"I got a final confirmation from all of our guests," Elsa said. "Everyone is safe at home and accounted for. And everyone thanks us for our commitment to their safety."

"I guess that's it, then." Nancy felt strangely hollow after the events of the previous few days. Perhaps it was just exhaustion. She closed her eyes and thought again about calling the doctor's office. They had stated the results would be in soon, but that was before anyone knew the storm was about to hit the island and, of course, had pushed everything back.

The waiting game only upped her anxiety.

"I think we should order food," Elsa suggested. "I don't feel like cooking."

"Me neither," Janine agreed.

"Pizza?" Mallory tried.

"We've had pizza so much lately," Carmella offered doubtfully.

"Does that mean you're against it?" Janine asked.

"Never. Not in a million years," Carmella affirmed with a playful smile. "Just wondered if we should cast any judgment on ourselves."

"Nope, not this week," Elsa said as she lifted her phone to dial their favorite place. "Carbs for days, please."

* * *

Henry's footage was featured on all major news stations over the next few days. Nancy sat at the edge of the couch alongside Mallory, Elsa, and Janine and watched herself as she described the damage the Katama Lodge had sustained and how she prayed for others on the island who had experienced so much more loss.

"Why did you let me wear my hair like that?" Nancy demanded of Janine.

Janine's lips parted in shock. "What are you talking about? You look beautiful."

Nancy rolled her eyes. "I have a face for radio."

"Good grief," Mallory said. "You're hot."

"See? You have confirmation from a twenty-four-year-old," Janine pointed out. "No more putting yourself down."

Nancy marveled yet again that you could be so far on your self-love journey and still not be anywhere at all. It was a lifelong job.

Henry's footage continued across the island. It showed the busted-up result of The Hesson House, along with a tearful Olivia Hesson, who explained that she'd received the mansion from her great aunt. "It was a beautiful dream, and maybe today, I have to put that dream to rest," she said.

Nancy wandered into the kitchen to find Carmella and Elsa, both hovering over the pile of dishes from breakfast. They'd taken to eating as a family as much as they could, especially in the wake of the hurricane— all of them gathered together over pancakes, sausages, eggs, and biscuits, contemplating just how lucky they were as the island continued to recuperate. It would be a long road ahead of them for sure.

And, of course, Nancy's test results hovered over them like more dark clouds. Everyone was on the verge of crumbling, it seemed like. The world could turn to chaos at any moment.

"You want help with these dishes?" Nancy asked now, sliding a hand across Carmella's shoulder lovingly.

Carmella exhaled and turned on the faucet. "No way. You know your only duty today is to rest."

Nancy laughed, although she didn't fully believe her humor. Elsa grabbed a large towel and began to dry the dishes as Carmella passed them over to her. Her eyes were shadowed.

"I spoke with Stan this morning," she announced.

"How is he doing?"

"He's thrilled to be at the Lodge, that's for sure," Elsa told her. "He took the smallest room. God bless him. But he also showed me the state of his house."

Nancy scrunched her nose. "That bad?"

"He said his son Tommy plans to help him with all repairs. They should be done in two months or so."

"That's fine."

Elsa nodded firmly. "He said he wants to give back as much as he can. I set him to work repainting that far wall in the kitchen. I figured it was best to get it done before the new guests arrive this weekend."

"Good thought. Maybe we could even hire him part-time after he returns home? The poor guy. I don't think I've spent more than five minutes with him in the past. When I got to the island, all I ever knew was that everyone hated him and kept their distance. But God knows he's not made any more mistakes than the rest of us."

Carmella paused and then turned off the water for a moment. "I still remember Anna Sheridan. I remember her as this beautiful angel, always quick to laugh, always giving us little pieces of candy when she ran into us. She died when I was maybe around fifteen?

Something like that? Gosh, around the time our mom died."

Elsa pressed her lips together. "The island felt shrouded in tragedy at the time. I remember thinking that death was, even more, a part of life than, well, living was."

"That's such a difficult thing for a teenager to face," Nancy breathed.

"It's just natural that we didn't have much compassion for Stan Ellis at the time," Carmella countered. "But now that he saved our lives during the hurricane, I've given real thought to how lonely that man has probably been over the years. The Lodge is practically perfect for him. He needs it much more than a lot of the women who pass through do."

Nancy's phone began to buzz. She lifted it from her robe pocket, then returned it. She didn't recognize the number and knew better than to answer strangers. But in a few moments, the phone rang again, and her curiosity flourished.

"Whoever that is, they really want to chat," Elsa teased.

"I'll just tell them I don't want whatever they're selling," Nancy said as she lifted her phone once again. "Hello, this is Nancy Remington speaking."

For a sharp, strange moment, silence filled the other end. Nancy's instinct told her to remove the phone from her ear and end the conversation. But just as she drew the phone from her ear, a voice rang out— powerful, confident, and terrifically hot.

"Nancy Remington. I wondered if I would ever hear that voice again."

It was as though a hand wrapped itself around Nancy's heart and stopped its beating. Then with a jolt, she remembered those eyes along the darkness of the waterline that night of her granddaughter's wedding. Maddox had awakened something within her that she'd long since put to rest. He had reminded her that she wasn't dead, not yet. So naturally, she'd assumed that he had run off the island, never to think of her again. Yet here he was.

"Maddox, I presume?"

"Oh, you're presuming, now? I thought that was only something Bond girls did," Maddox teased her.

Nancy's heart now quickened to the speed of a rabbit's.

"What can I do for you, Maddox?"

Both Elsa and Carmella had yanked themselves around to gape at their stepmother. Carmella mouthed, "The guy from the wedding?" while Elsa pressed her hands together and did a little dance. Nancy playfully scowled at them and turned toward the window. She had to remain cool and calculated.

"I happened to just be flicking through the news here in the city. Then low and behold, a beautiful woman I met at a wedding appeared on my screen. It felt like fate."

"You know better than to believe in fate," Nancy told him.

"Do I? Because I think I'd rather live in a world where I believe in all of that stuff. Fate. Destiny."

"I never imagined you to be anything but pragmatic," Nancy told him.

"You'd better start thinking of me differently, Nancy Remington."

"And why is that?"

"Because I'd like to ask you out. That's why."

Nancy's heart leaped into her throat. She jumped

around and gaped at her stepdaughters, now totally at a loss. She felt like a middle schooler, without a single experience under her belt. Sometimes men who mattered made you feel that way; she knew that. Or she'd once known that.

Plus, in the wake of all those tests, she'd never envisioned that anyone would ever ask her out again. Not in this life, at least.

"How did you get my number?" Nancy asked, careful to keep her voice measured.

"I have my ways. I'm a very rich and connected man."

"You say that as though I should be impressed," Nancy returned.

At this, Maddox erupted with laughter. "I say it because I know you aren't. You're much too clever for something like that."

"You hardly know me," Nancy said softly now. She leaned against the cool wall of the kitchen and, for the first time, allowed herself to dream.

"Just tell me you'll meet me in three days," Maddox told her. "Tell me you'll give me a single chance to show you something amazing. You deserve it after everything you've been through."

"And what do you get out of it?"

"Probably nothing," Maddox said. "Just the pleasure of a very beautiful and intelligent woman's company. I don't know that there's much more in this life to look for."

When Nancy hung up the phone, both Elsa and Carmella screeched with such overzealous joy that Janine hustled into the room, fully panicked, her eyes nearly popping from her skull.

"What is it?" she demanded.

Nancy clutched her phone to her chest. She hardly had words, so Carmella explained.

"I assumed he'd forgotten all about me," Nancy stuttered.

"Nancy. How could that ever happen?" Elsa said with a laugh. "You're one of the most memorable creatures on this planet, with more stories than you even know what to do with. Maddox is lucky you've agreed to share air with him a second time. You know that."

Chapter Twenty-One

The late September sunlight peeked through a faraway cloud. Nancy stood in a fluttering cream-colored blouse on the far end of the Edgartown docks as the breeze swept through her hair. Only five minutes before, she and Janine had hovered in Janine's car as Nancy had smeared the last of her lipstick over her lips and inspected her reflection in the mirror.

"Ridiculous. I haven't been on a date in over twelve years," she'd said, mostly to herself.

"You'll call me if you need anything?"

"Look at us. We've reversed roles," Nancy had teased before she'd leaped out into the glow of the seventy-degree, late September day. "I'll see you later, Jan. Don't stay up for me." She'd winked playfully like a teenager up to no good.

"I'm getting bad flashbacks of Alyssa and Maggie's high school years," Janine had laughed as she'd turned on the engine and eased slowly down the road.

Maddox had orchestrated a plan for the day ahead. This seemed very much up his alley. He was the sort of man who knew what he wanted, when he wanted it, and had the money to back up his every whim. Now, for whatever reason, Nancy had aligned with his current "whims." She gripped the railing on the docks as her eyes scanned the horizon. "I'll sail in like some kind of pirate and whisk you off to undiscovered lands," he'd told her on the phone the previous evening. She'd teased him about this afterward. "Will you be wearing an eye patch? Will you make me walk the plank? Should I turn you into the relevant authorities? I'm pretty sure pirating isn't legal."

But when his boat appeared, Nancy's heart thudded on warp speed. He stood out on the bow of the boat in a navy blue jacket, a pair of white slacks and perfect boat shoes. The wind caught his salt-and-pepper hair beautifully, and his smile glowed with a mix of adventure and secrecy. Nancy was reminded of old books she'd read as a child— ones that had described scenes just like this where the man whisks woman off to greater lands beyond her wildest dreams.

"You're a sight for sore eyes," she told him.

Maddox laughed. It was a ridiculously handsome laugh. Someone should have recorded it and sold it.

"Let me help you," Maddox said, splaying his hand out as the boat bumped against the dock. Nancy slid her hand into his and allowed him to guide her into the belly of the boat. She'd gone sailing countless times with Neal over the years and found herself immediately trusting Maddox's instincts on his own boat. Neal had taught her enough that she immediately fell into action. Maddox whistled, clearly impressed.

"Somebody's done this before," he said.

Nancy hovered near the stern and adjusted one of the sails as they whipped out away from the docks and headed for the open waters of the Nantucket Sound. "I'm no islander, but I've been trained in the art of the lifestyle."

"I have a feeling you're that type of woman. You can fit wherever you want to fit," Maddox offered.

Nancy beamed as she considered this. She could now visualize herself in countless locations during various eras across her life: Nancy in Bangkok, on the adventure of a lifetime; Nancy as a young mother, seventeen and with hardly two pennies to rub together; Nancy out on the open road, her heart shattered in a million pieces as she left her daughter behind.

And now— this version of Nancy held a potentially life-threatening illness, yes, but she was also a brave version. One that was open to the opportunity of spending a glorious day with this handsome stranger. Somehow, despite what she'd told him about her fears of the unknown, he had remembered her enough to want to include her in another era of his own life.

For a long time, Maddox and Nancy were both so focused on the intricacies of sailing that they didn't say anything but the necessary dialogue two sailors needed to make it across the waves. When they reached a calm spot on the western side of the island, near the Aquinnah Cliffs Overlook, Maddox stalled the sails and dropped himself against the edge of the sailboat so that his toes skimmed the water.

"Wild to me that autumn is here," he said. "But the air is beautiful today. Almost good enough for a swim."

"Almost?" Nancy waggled her eyebrows and then whipped off her dress to reveal her one-piece suit beneath. She then squeezed her nose and dropped into the water. There was just soft, dark silence as she sank down and down into the depths of the Vineyard Sound. Years ago, she and Neal had had a small competition to see how long they could hold their breaths. They'd dunked themselves down in the water just off Neal's mansion and held one another's hands as they'd shifted around in the darkness, their eyes closed against the salt. Now, as Nancy dropped down and down, her eyes closed again, she searched for some sign of Neal around her. Was he watching her? Did he know how much she dreamed of him?

A bit after that, there was an eruption through the waves as Maddox leaped in. This tore through Nancy's reverie. She swam up toward the light and burst up, flashing her hair behind her. When she caught her breath and opened her eyes, she found Maddox's beautiful eyes peering back at her just above the surface of the water. She had the sudden desire to fling herself into his arms and kiss him with reckless abandon. Something held her back, though.

Maddox gripped the railing of the boat. His muscles bulged out over the waves as he regarded her. Nancy continued to tread water, grateful for her strength.

"It's a funny thing to meet someone like you so late in my life," Maddox said.

Nancy couldn't speak. Everything felt tremendously heavy.

"Maybe it would be easier for me if I could pretend we had all the time in the world," he continued.

"What would we do with all that time?" Nancy asked.

"Well, since we're twenty-five, we're a bit reckless with ourselves," Maddox said.

"Sounds about right."

"One day, I come home to our rickety apartment..."

"It's cockroach infested, I assume?"

"Oh yes. We can't get rid of them," Maddox affirmed. "And I come home to find you there, and you tell me you're tired of the city, tired of seeing all the same old people all the time. You're tired of the same old humdrum conversations. And you look at me and you kiss me and you say, Maddox, take me away from this place."

"Oh, do I?"

"You do. So we pack up a little suitcase, drop it in the trunk of my convertible—"

"How can you afford a convertible? Shouldn't we have upgraded apartments by now?" Nancy asked.

"My father gave it to me when he disappeared with that gang of circus performers, and I can't bear to part with it," Maddox explained.

"Oh, of course. I understand."

"Plus, there's no way I'm taking the beautiful Nancy Remington across the country in anything but this baby-blue convertible. Even in the first stretch of our journey, I get jealous of everyone for looking at you. Everyone flirts with you: the gas station attendant, the owner of the diner, even the guy who helps us change a tire on the side of the road. And you're just so charming that you can't help it. The world just wants to wait on you, hand and foot."

Nancy's grin widened. She loved living in his daydream. She could have fallen into its light for the rest of her days.

"Where do we go?"

"We drive from the city to Memphis, Tennessee, because you tell me your first love was Elvis, and I want to show you I care," Maddox continued. "We arrive at

Graceland, and I ask you to marry me outside beneath the shimmering Tennessee sun, and you tell me no, not yet. I know you'll make a game out of this. You'll make me ask you over and over again. And I tell you I'm ready to do it. I'm ready to go to the ends of the earth if only you decide to spend the rest of your days with me."

Nancy cackled. "I never took you for a big romantic."

"Oh, but I am. And I load you back in the blue convertible, and we drive onward toward the Rocky Mountains. In Denver, we climb to the top of a mountain and up there, again, I ask you to marry me. Again, you say no, but I can see it in your eyes. I'm wearing you down."

"Probably. I'm just annoyed with you."

"Maybe so, but what else can you do? I'm your only ride."

"I'm sure I could make a new life here in Denver," Nancy teased. "I could marry a bar owner or a businessman or a mountaineer."

"You really could. We both know that. And we're only twenty-five with our whole lives ahead of us. I know I have to work every day to convince you to stay with me for the rest of our days. But I'm ready for it."

Nancy laughed again. He continued his story—stretching them all the way to the Pacific Ocean, where a gang of circus performers steals his car, and they eventually meet up with his father, who has mastered the art of the trapeze and teaches Maddox how. Up there on the high wire, he calls down to Nancy and asks her, yet again, to marry him. Yet again, Nancy says no.

"I'm really at the end of my rope at this point. But then, one morning, you turn to me and tell me that you're pregnant, and I know I've got you once and for all. I'll show you and our baby that I can be the best man in the world. And we'll raise our child on the open road, open-minded and open to endless possibilities."

Nancy allowed the silence to fill the space between them. Her heart thudded loudly beneath the calm waters. She finally gripped the edge of the sailboat, suddenly exhausted.

"It's a beautiful story," she said.

"It's a real story," Maddox said. "In another reality—another life."

Nancy wasn't sure why, but she wanted to cry. She pulled herself out of the water and wrapped herself in a towel. Maddox joined her. He grabbed a bottle of wine from a cooler and poured them both glasses. When Nancy drew up the courage to look into his eyes again, she saw a hint of loneliness.

"Did you ever find someone to have that kind of story with?" she asked him as the waves gently knocked against the boat.

Maddox's eyes grew shadowed. "I think I was too proud to ever fall in love properly. I was obsessed with my career. I was obsessed with status. So I never learned how to be intimate with anyone. Maybe I regret it. I don't know. But I suppose you can't regret anything because you don't know how different your life might have been."

Nancy sipped her wine and blinked out across the waves. She then inched her way toward Maddox, who drew his large legs out on either side of him and allowed her to lean her back against his chest. She was tucked safely in his arms as they shared a vision of a false reality — nothing they could ever have, which was all the more beautiful because of its fiction.

"I'm really glad you called me," Nancy said as Maddox filled their glasses again with wine. "Knowing you for this brief time has reminded me of something within myself. Something I thought I'd lost a long time ago."

Maddox considered this. "I feel the same. You know that I've worked with your ex-son-in-law a great deal. It seems like men like Jack in the city are a dime a dozen. Cruel men who've been handed every good card in the deck. Yes, I've been lucky, but I've been grateful for all of it. And I'm grateful now to see this other side of life— something bigger and grander and more meaningful. I don't know what happens next. I don't know if you ever want to see me again. But if you want to explore these newfound elements of ourselves together—"

Nancy's heart felt squeezed. Everything in the world now weighed heavily on the results of her medical tests.

But instead of pointing to this ominous fear, she just nodded. She smiled and felt a glow of youth and vitality fall through her.

"I would like that," she whispered. "And maybe, if it doesn't work out, we can have a wild and rash breakup. A public one. Screaming in the streets."

"Like teenagers. Yes," Maddox said, stringing his fingers through hers. "Now you understand. I just want a dramatic story."

"I think I can do that for you," Nancy whispered. She then leaned her head back heavily against his chest and listened to the soft bump-bump of his sixty-year-old heart. Time was unkind, but it was also beautiful in its earnest ability to teach you who you really were and what you really wanted. Nancy promised herself to squeeze whatever life she could out of the moments she had left. It was all she could do.

Chapter Twenty-Two

Nancy and Janine sat in the front seat of Janine's car about a block away from the Oak Bluffs ferry dock. The engine hummed, and the radio flicked and spat with the weather report. Above, clouds grew ominous, curling into gray and tapping down big raindrops over the windshield. It wouldn't be a tropical storm, just a healthy autumn rain. Nancy exhaled all the air from her lungs and then reminded herself to keep breathing. Within the next eight hours, she would know the truth.

Everything always happened at once. The previous night, Maggie had called Janine to say she was back from honeymoon number one and wanted to come down for a visit. Of course, Alyssa wanted to tag along, as well. "Are you already sick of being married?" Nancy had asked when the phone had been passed to her. Maggie had just laughed and said, "I swear, he snores more than he used to now. Should I get the marriage annulled?"

Nobody said anything about it, but Nancy felt pretty sure that her granddaughters wanted to return to the island because of the incoming test results. News of this had had everyone on edge. Janine had only picked at her food the previous few nights. Her wine pours had been extra healthy, as well. The conversation hadn't flowed with its usual easy, lovely energy. Instead, it had faltered and drawn itself into silences.

"I still can't believe you went on such a romantic date with Maddox," Janine said now as she clicked the radio off. "The way Jack used to talk about him, I never imagined him to be such a romantic."

"It doesn't sound like he reveals his true self to most people," Nancy told her.

Janine considered this. "You always had that way with people. I remember as a kid, feeling like everyone from the bodega owner to the bartender at the local bar just looked at you differently and treated you differently. Like you were made of magic." She chuckled to herself. "I thought you were made of magic, too."

"You were wrong," Nancy said softly. "Just old bones and muscle, like everyone else."

"If I know one thing, it's that my mother isn't like everyone else," Janine said pointedly, making heavy eye contact. "Maybe she's a little messy, a little all over the place. Maybe she loves a little too hard. Maybe she hasn't made every good decision in the book. But she's lived a wide-open and free life. And isn't that more than most people could ever ask for?"

Nancy blinked back tears. She placed her hand over Janine's and tried to come up with the right words to say—words that would eliminate the fear that permeated between them. The fear of the unknown. Nancy had watched Neal die; she would have given anything to take that sort of thing away from Janine.

Janine had been her first love. She was her forever love.

"There's the ferry." Janine reached back for a large umbrella, then slid out to trace a path over to Nancy's side. Nancy jumped under her umbrella as the two hustled over to the ferry.

"Do you remember sharing an umbrella in New York with me?" Nancy asked as they raced along. "We always jumped through puddles, which kind of made the umbrella thing silly. We were always soaked clean through by the end."

Alyssa and Maggie appeared at the top of the ferry and waved down beneath their umbrellas. Both wore this year's iconic Prada collection along with glorious rain boots and perfect fall hats. Nancy was continually stunned by their fashion sensibilities. Janine liked to tell her that Alyssa and Maggie had learned from Janine, who'd taken everything she'd learned from Nancy. Nancy had had to put together her fashion sense with "whatever she found along the way."

"There she is! My married daughter," Janine said as she hugged Maggie beneath the umbrella, careful to keep it upright over herself and Nancy.

"And your unmarried one!" Alyssa said, beaming. "Completely single and loving it."

"She's only saying that because she wants to talk all about how Peter is begging her to get back together," Maggie said with a roll of her eyes.

"And why won't you?" Janine asked.

Alyssa shrugged.

"She likes the game too much," Maggie said.

"I can understand that," Nancy affirmed as she placed

a hand over Alyssa's shoulder. "The game is almost enough, isn't it?"

Alyssa's smile widened. "I knew Grandma would get it. She's the only one who takes any real risks around here."

"Mom said you had a little sailing adventure with Maddox?" Maggie asked coyly.

Nancy laughed and dropped her head back. Joy permeated through her muscles; her cheeks ached with her grin.

"She's not going to tell us what happened," Alyssa said, aghast. "She's going to keep it to herself."

"Mom, what happened at the end of the sailing trip?" Janine asked as they stepped back toward the car.

Nancy shook her head. "A lady never reveals her secrets."

"You're no lady," Janine quipped. "You're Nancy Grimson. You're an icon."

What had she and Maddox done? The thought of it thrilled her. She put herself back in that story as she sat at the edge of the couch back at the house, her hands clutching her knees tightly. As usual, Maggie and Alyssa had dragged several suitcases of clothes along with them to the Vineyard. Even now, they splayed out some of their new outfits to show off for their mother and grandmother. Maggie had countless stories about her honeymoon, which she shared now.

"We panicked one night because Rex has a peanut allergy, and we were sure he'd eaten something with peanut sauce," she said. "We rushed to the hospital and ordered that he be taken care of. But then we waited, and nothing happened."

"Then tell them what you did after that," Alyssa urged, wagging her eyebrows.

Maggie's cheeks brightened to crimson. "Well, we wandered down the hallway to a supplies closet."

"Maggie!" Janine cried.

Nancy clapped her hands joyously. "You're a married woman, Maggie. And you've already discovered the first thing about marriage. You have to mix it up with surprises; otherwise, it gets stale."

Janine shook her head wildly. "I don't believe this. So you're condoning this kind of behavior?"

"Absolutely. One hundred percent." Nancy nodded with a wide grin.

Alyssa and Maggie held one another and cackled.

"Grandma, you should write a book," Maggie suggested as her laughter subsided. "I know tons of women in their twenties who lack the spirit you have. Maybe you could sell it to them."

"A fifty-nine-year-old woman at the top of her game," Alyssa agreed.

Nancy's smile faltered. Her eyes scanned toward the phone, which remained silent. Had the doctor already looked at the test results? Did he plan to wait till after lunch, before dinner? When would the call come?

It was good to distract themselves. It was one, and Alyssa drew out a bottle of French wine that Maggie had brought from her honeymoon. She popped it open and poured them each a glass. Alyssa and Maggie sat on the ground and crossed their legs, demanding still more stories from Nancy about her life around the world. In turn, Nancy demanded more about Maggie's honeymoon.

When Maggie spoke of Rex, it was as though her eyes formed into glowing clouds; her hands scattered around her like butterflies as she explained each tale. In everything she did, she exuded love for him.

"You remind me of the way I was after I met Neal," Nancy said quietly. "You know that love has given you this impossible strength."

Maggie nodded as her smile faltered. "It's like you're flying and praying all the time that you'll never fall."

"You won't fall. Not as long as you believe in what you're doing, in what you have."

The call came just after three-thirty. Nancy had drunk two and a half glasses of French wine by then. She felt giddy and strange but oddly calm. When she lifted the phone, she exhaled and said, "Hello, Doctor. Get me out of this not-knowing baloney. I'm so tired of not knowing."

The doctor cackled. The laughter had nothing to do with any somber realities. Instead, it was like a song.

"Nancy Remington, you're going to be just fine. I'm going to put you on medicine to balance out some of your hormones; I think that's why you've been so tired lately. It happens. Our bodies can go out of whack like that. I'm also going to suggest some B12 shots as well."

Nancy's lips parted in disbelief. "That's it?"

"Yes. All your tests came back normal. You're still almost a portrait of health, just like I always said. But again, I'm sorry it took so long to get back to you. The hurricane really threw us for a loop."

"Us too," Nancy said. "The whole island, I guess."

"I'm going to pass you over to the secretary to make preparations for another appointment: next week or something. We'll get to the bottom of this fatigue problem and get you back out and about. We all know you're just about as fiery as ever. I'm not even sure we should fix you up, to be honest. You might go out on another adventure and never see us again," the doctor continued.

Nancy laughed. Beside her, Maggie and Alyssa and Janine had caught on to the fact that Nancy would be all right. They huddled around her and hugged her close as the doctor's secretary made plans for the next week. When she dropped the phone to the side, Nancy placed her head tenderly on Maggie's shoulder and let herself cry for the first time that day. It felt like the ultimate release— like the air being let out of something so full it was on the verge of combustion.

The pressure was gone now, though.

She was going to live.

Suddenly, at fifty-nine, the winds had returned to her sails. Whatever she could dream about could be possible. The time now belonged to her. And she would be brave enough to fly.

Coming next in the Katama Bay Series

Read A Thanksgiving Full of Gratitude

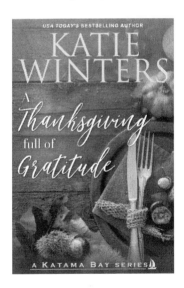

Other Books by Katie

The Vineyard Sunset Series

Sisters of Edgartown Series

Secrets of Mackinac Island Series

A Katama Bay Series

A Mount Desert Island Series

A Nantucket Sunset Series

Made in the USA
Middletown, DE
01 November 2024

63716054R00106